Panhandlers
A Novel in Stories

Nic Schuck

Panhandlers
A Novel in Stories

ISBN: 978-1-63795-353-2

Copyright © 2018

Panhandle Books

"I now must change those notes to tragic; foul distrust, and breach disloyal on the part of Man, revolt, and disobedience …"

— John Milton, Paradise Lost

"Wisdom came to live among men and found no dwelling place."

— Book of Enoch

To Zoe

Table of Contents

Can't Take Nothing with You 1
Puerto Rico, Revised 12
The Defeated 33
White Tropic Dreams... 50
Teacher of the Year 98
Roulette... 113
Summer Songlines.. 116
Alright Guy... 147
Fly, Brother, Fly!... 169
Saga of Milt Andrews... 188
Southern Cross 200
Merle 220
Acknowledgments 239
Author Bio 240

Can't Take Nothing with You

"Boy, take care of your brother today. You hear me?"

Teddy Ackerman had plans already and babysitting wasn't one of them. Hank liked it though. He would go to the pool hall with his older brother and play pinball while Teddy hustled the older boys. Teddy would buy Hank a pack of baseball cards with some of the winnings. He always did. When Teddy chopped wood for burger money, Hank collected rocks. Or they could find a yard to rake leaves and earn money for ammunition to go shooting. Whatever money Teddy earned, Hank knew some of it would be spent on a good time. Teddy always said, "Can't take nothing with you when you go."

Teddy recently started doing something different, which earned him more money than any of his other jobs, and this new endeavor was something he didn't want little Hank to see.

Teddy was seventeen and didn't know much, but what he did know was that he didn't want to clean pools like his old man. At season's end, his dad had to find other work. That was what his dad was supposed to be doing today, looking for work to get him and his boys through the winter. Teddy knew how it would probably go, though. After about two hours of talking to different people, he would stop at the gas station for a beer and then maybe find a poker game or dice game and he would continue drinking until late at night or the early morning hours. After a few weeks, he would ride into town to the unemployment office and live off the little bit the government gave him. He received just enough to keep the pantry filled with Ramen noodles and the refrigerator filled with Milwaukee's Best beer, or as he called it, The Beast.

Teddy saved enough to buy a pick-up truck, an '86 Ford F-150 with the gear shift on the steering column and 156,000 miles on it. He found it in Auto Trader for two hundred and fifty dollars. To get it running, he gave it what he called a quick tune up—replaced the spark plugs, changed out the radiator with one he pulled from a junk yard, new belts, and rebuilt the carburetor. He worked on it for nearly six months and was pleased when he finished. Then he worked on the body, hammering out dints and sanding off most of the rust. He figured it would take about another three weeks before it would look somewhat presentable to the ladies in the Cosmetology Department of the vocational school just fifty miles south in Pensacola. He planned on attending there one day to learn to fix air-conditioners. He heard there was good money in heating and air.

After Teddy Sr. left, Hank complained he was hungry. Teddy looked in the pantry—can of baked beans with bacon, some creamed corn, and a bag of rice. The fridge wasn't any better—some chunky milk, two eggs, a potato, a tomato, and a coffee cup of solid bacon fat. He rinsed out the iron skillet that was still dirty from three or four days ago when he cooked sloppy joes. He cut the potato into thin slices and fried the slices in the bacon grease. He cracked the eggs over the fried potato and then added the diced tomato in with it. He seasoned it with salt and pepper packets from Whataburger before serving it to Hank. Teddy ate beans straight from the can that he opened with his pocket knife.

It took three tries before the exhaust spit out a cloud of black smoke and the engine came alive. He spun his tires as he left the gravel driveway and smiled when his little brother giggled. Hank called it "doing a Dukes of Hazzard." Teddy, from his rearview mirror, watched the dog come from underneath the trailer. He couldn't believe that his dad was sixty-four years old and never owned his own house.

The trailer wasn't really a trailer but an old wooden camp car from the 1920s that was left over from the lumber industry in Sullivan, Florida, a small town just below the Alabama line. The camp car sat on a piece of land that had been cleared of all the virgin longleaf pines and was sold for farming and was now owned by Teddy's dad's one-time employer at the sand company and very little farming happened anymore. Teddy's dad hadn't worked for Rafferty's Sand Company for years. They couldn't let him drive the trucks after his second DUI. But when Teddy Sr.'s wife died of breast cancer and Mr. Rafferty saw those two little boys and the life they were destined to live, he didn't have the heart to evict them when rent payments started coming in less and less. He was lucky if he saw six payments a year. He figured it wasn't hurting anything. The trailer didn't really cost him much to keep there.

"Where we going today, Teddy?"

"We can go to Rodney's and ride his go-karts later. But I gotta get some money first."

"Cutting grass today?"

Teddy shook his head.

"Playing pool?"

Teddy shook his head.

"Painting?"

Teddy shook his head. "I got something else. Look kid, when we get to this place just stay in the truck, all right? You can't come in."

"Why?"

"I gotta do something that you shouldn't see."

"Why?"

"It just isn't good for a kid your age to see. But it makes me a lot of money, sometimes."

"That's how you bought the truck?"

"Yeah."

"What is it?"

"Chicken fights."

"Like we do at the lake?"

Teddy laughed.

"No, we use real chickens. You bet on which one wins."

Hank looked at his brother. "How do you get the chickens to stay on your shoulders?"

"Not like that, stupid. The chickens are on the ground and they fight each other."

After a while, Hank said, "Oh" and then asked, "Why can't I see it?"

"Maybe when you're older."

"Okay." Hank stuck his hand out the window, moving his hand up and down like a snake flying in the wind.

They pulled up to a barn that looked like if someone

were to lean on it too hard it would fall over. There were twenty or so cars, trucks, tractors, and even a lawnmower parked alongside of it.

"Remember just stay here. You hear me?"

Hank nodded.

Inside, men hollered and shouted and pushed each other to get a better look. Teddy went to the makeshift ticket counter where he could place his bets.

"Hold your money, boy. We got something better coming up. Trust me," Lenny Jr. said. He was a lanky man with a graying beard that nearly reached his belly and a gray, braided ponytail that nearly reached his ass and most people never saw him in anything except a black Stetson, black boots, and a black vest.

Teddy watched four cock fights, itching to get in on the action. But when Lenny Jr. gave advice, he took it. The last of the cock fights took place and the losers went home. The winners stuck around to see Lenny Jr.'s surprise.

Lenny Jr. put a megaphone to his mouth and said, "Bring 'em out, boys."

Four men left the barn and came back with growling, slobbering, muzzled dogs. There were two Pit-bulls, a Rottweiler, and a German Sheppard. The gamblers shouted in excitement. Lenny Jr. hosted dog fights a few years back, but when people started reporting their dogs missing, he laid low a while. Some of the county police knew about the dog fights, even participated, but when people started to steal dogs for blood sport, it was time for Lenny Jr. to stop. He switched to cock fights. Now the time was right when they could go back to the big money games.

Lenny Jr.'s dog fights weren't the kind of dog fights you read about in the papers. His fights were just people's dogs that were mean and would fight. Sure, people would do things to make their dogs more aggressive, but it wasn't to the point of sport where they would run them on a tread mill with a chain around their neck. It was just dogs fighting. Sometimes they wouldn't fight, but most times they did.

Lenny Jr. put a hand on Teddy's shoulder. "Your daddy still got that old mean sumbitch around?" he asked. "You know, if you bring a dog, you get a ten-percent cut from the house. Fifteen if your dog wins."

Teddy looked up at him.

"That means whether your dog wins or loses, you still win. You don't even have to bet if you don't wanna."

"He's pretty old," Teddy said.

"Don't matter. We just need dogs."

The first two matches were over. Teddy lost one-hundred dollars, fifty on each fight. Lenny Jr. allowed the dogs' owners to throw in the towel whenever they wanted. That didn't always sit too well with the betters. Sometimes the dog fights led to fist fights. Lenny Jr. made them take it outside. But he still took bets, on the dogs and the men.

After the dogs, the cock fights resumed. The men wanted more dogs, though. Cocks just weren't the same. Not as much blood. Not as much noise. Lenny Jr. wanted more dogs, too. Cocks weren't as much money.

He went back to Teddy, "What do you say?"

"I'll be back."

Hank was asleep in the truck bed. "Get up. We gotta go back to the house."

"We gonna ride go-karts?"

"Not yet."

"What're we gonna do?"

"Get Shithead."

"Taking him to the lake?"

"Nah."

Shithead was a mix of German Sheppard and Black Lab with paws like a bear and years ago he was a fierce creature.

Teddy crawled under the trailer and grabbed Shithead by the collar and dragged him out. Shithead growled and barked, but he knew better than to bite Teddy. Hank got out of the truck to pet the old dog. The dog snapped at him and Teddy popped him across the snout. Then he lifted him into the bed.

"Can I ride back here with him?" Hank asked.

"If you want. He probably stinks."

"I don't care none if he stinks."

Shithead circled around before lying down. Hank remembered after his momma died, he used to lay with his head on the dog's belly. As Shithead got older, he got meaner and Hank didn't remember the last time Shithead was out from under the house.

"Stay in the truck," Teddy said when they got back to the barn. Shithead barked when he saw the barn.

"What are you gonna do with Shithead?"

"Nothing."

"Then why did you bring him here?"

"Shut up. Stay in the truck like I said. You want to ride go-karts or what? I gotta buy some gas if we do. Rodney ain't gonna let us use his."

Hank had a vague memory of when he was younger and his dad would go for a ride with Shithead, and the dog would come back bloodied and lame. It usually took a couple weeks before he was back to his old self. Hank didn't like that and was glad when his dad stopped doing it. He was never given an explanation as to what happened.

"It'll be all right, boy," Hank told the dog.

The dog looked up at him. He knew better and lunged at Hank. Teddy yanked on the choke chain around Shithead's neck and stopped the dog from mauling his little brother.

"Good boy," Lenny Jr. said walking out to the truck.

Shithead snapped at Lenny Jr. Teddy didn't swat him this time.

"Still vicious, huh?" Lenny Jr. said.

Teddy nodded. But he knew better. It was all show. The damn dog was too old.

"This one used to be a killer. I seen him this one time bite a big ol' Chow on the back of the neck, plop his paws down on him, and snap it like a matchstick. Your old man won a lot of money with this one. Hope he still gots it in him."

"How much I get?"

"I give it to ya at the end of the day."

Lenny Jr. looked at Hank. "The kid can't come in."

"He's gonna stay here. Ain't ya?"

Hank nodded.

Hank sat in the truck trying to hold back tears as he

watched Teddy struggling with Shithead on the walk to the barn.

Shithead's opponent was the Rottweiler from earlier, one that lost. The pit-bulls only fought other pit-bulls. Teddy walked Shithead to the ring. The crowd was loud and Teddy could feel the pulse of the crowd mixed with his own heartbeat. He felt as if he were the one about to step into the ring. The Rottweiler was muzzled, but when the muzzle was taken off, the dog went ape-shit.

"Just remember, you can stop this whenever you want," Lenny Jr. told him.

Teddy nodded.

"Let's fight," Lenny Jr. shouted into the megaphone.

The two owners unhooked the leashes. The dogs sprinted to mid-ring. It was a good battle for the first minute, but then Shithead began to tire. The two dogs separated under their own terms. Shithead didn't have all of one of his ears anymore. The two animals stood in a stare-down. Shithead lowered his head and licked the blood that streamed down into his mouth from his ear.

"You wanna stop it?" Lenny Jr. asked. "He ain't looking too good."

Teddy shook his head. He wanted to paint the truck. "I think he can do it," he said. The dog didn't have many days ahead of him anyway.

In an instant, the Rottweiler leapt at Shithead. Shithead lunged for a counter-attack, but the Rottweiler was too quick. His mouth clamped shut just under Shithead's jowls and sunk his teeth into Shithead's throat. The two owners rushed to the center. The other owner wedged a short, but thick, solid ax handle between Shithead's neck and his dog's mouth. After the third yank, he pried the dogs apart. Shithead lay motionless. Teddy stood over him.

"Get him outta here," Lenny Jr. said.

Teddy picked him up and walked him through the murmuring crowd. Lenny Jr. stopped him and placed a hundred-dollar bill into his shirt pocket and said something to him, but Teddy wasn't listening.

He stepped out into the early autumn afternoon and felt the first bit of chill in the air in nearly seven months. The sky remained overcast throughout the day and reminded everyone that the long Florida summer was over. The end of the week even called for a freeze warning.

Teddy looked out at the truck and saw that Hank wasn't waiting in the bed of the truck. He sat on top of two crates underneath a window, looking in the barn.

"Get over here," Teddy shouted.

Hank did as he was told.

"What'd I tell you?"

Hank didn't answer. He looked at Shithead. The hair around the dog's neck matted with blood. A couple holes looked big enough to stick his fingers in, kind of like a bowling ball. The rest looked like raw hamburger meat. Shithead tried to look up, but he struggled to open his eyes. The dog's head hung over Teddy's arms and he barely showed signs of breathing. Hank looked down at his feet and followed Teddy to the truck.

Teddy put the dog in the bed of the truck and then turned

and smacked Hank in the back of the head when his hands were free. "I told you not to leave here."

Hank lifted a hand to rub the back of his head, but didn't say anything. He stood looking at the blood on his brother's shirt and then rubbed the back of his hand into his eye.

"None of that crying bullshit, ya hear me? He'll be all right."

"No, he won't," Hank said.

"You're probably right, but he was old anyway."

"Did you at least make any money?"

"Nah. Broke even. But sometimes that's just as good as winning."

Hank said nothing. He climbed into the bed with Shithead and laid his head on the animal's slow-breathing stomach.

"Hey, when pop comes home, don't say a word. All right? He can't know about this. He'll have both our asses."

Hank nodded.

On the drive home, Hank's head stopped rising and falling on the dog's stomach, but he lay like that until they made it to the house. Teddy looked at his little brother lying with the dead dog and allowed him to stay like that a little longer. His dad wouldn't be home for a few more hours and that left them with plenty of time to put the dog back underneath the house.

Puerto Rico, Revised

"I went to Puerto Rico and all I got was this fucked-up hand." That was what Teddy Ackerman said to Rodney Helms as he leaned over and showed Rodney his hand. He could no longer make a fist or straighten it out completely. His pinky and ring finger were permanently bent out of shape from a boxer's fracture.

They were on their fourth beer at a beach bar that was reportedly said to be the oldest bar on the island. A bar they made "their bar" by going there when Rodney made it back up to Pensacola. It had been about three years since he last visited. During that visit, Teddy and his wife had a newborn and Rodney didn't get to hang out with him like they wanted. Rodney went to Teddy's house, drank one beer, held the little boy, made some small talk, got bored and said, "See you later."

This time though, Teddy was divorced, and Rodney felt bad for him. Teddy was a good guy. But he got caught fooling around with a bartender at Trader Jon's, an aviator bar in Downtown Pensacola, and his wife wasn't having it. No second chances. He was pretty distraught about it. Really missed his boy. Only got to see him every other weekend and he already had a step-daddy, too. Rodney imagined how that must've stung a bit.

They laughed for some time after Teddy showed his hand. It was the first time they laughed that night and Rodney noticed how Teddy's eyes watered up as he laughed.

* * * *

After high school, Teddy and Rodney planned to take a surf trip somewhere, anywhere. But Rodney earned a full-ride scholarship to play third base for the Miami Hurricanes and the trip was postponed until after graduation. Rodney earned a degree in Athletics Training, didn't get drafted, but instead went to the Major League Scouting Bureau Tryout Camp in Tuscaloosa, Alabama. He didn't make the cut there either. He played in an adult league around town to keep in shape, but it was heartbreaking and Rodney carried that heartbreak with him on those beautiful spring days. He spent countless hours at the batting cages. Sometimes he was so drunk while trying to hit the balls that he'd miss every one of them, but other times, he hit what would be homeruns with every swing.

Rodney didn't have the cash or the heart for a surf trip that year and postponed it again. In the meantime, he took a job as an elementary school P.E. teacher. There were only three guys on the entire staff and most of the women were under forty-five so he told himself things could be worse. He went to the training camp again the following year and was cut for the second time, so still didn't have money for a surf trip. He decided that was what credit cards were for, and they took the trip in April during his second Spring Break as a teacher.

The timing worked out well because spring was the only time Teddy could get away. He worked at a heating and air company and was doing pretty well. He could get away in the early spring season when people didn't need heating nor air, but by summertime, he'd have to be in the truck running fourteen-hour days.

They tossed around ideas for where to go: El Salvador, Costa Rica, Panama, Nicaragua, and settled on Barbados after having watched a surf video that showcased Barbados's famed break, Soup Bowl. Teddy would have gone anywhere. It was really Rodney who made the decision, but after calling around on some prices, the eight-hundred-dollar plane ticket to Barbados was a bit out of the budget. They found tickets to Puerto Rico for only two hundred and fifty dollars, that's where they went.

Teddy drove down to Miami from Pensacola to spend a few days in South Florida before going on the trip. It was his first time leaving the Panhandle since that time he and Rodney were in high school and drove to Jacksonville in Teddy's rebuilt pick-up truck.

They sat in Teddy's rental car watching the Atlantic Ocean at Hollywood Beach. Teddy rolled up a second joint.

"When we come back I have to become a professional again, a role model. You believe that shit? I'm a teacher," Rodney said.

"Hell no. Tell you the truth, never thought you'd finish school."

"Thanks," Rodney said.

"I'm just saying."

"I guess you never thought I'd make it to the Majors either?"

"I always thought you would. Hoped you would, too."

"Anyway, we've got ten days, my brother."

Teddy handed Rodney the joint and Rodney stuck it behind his ear. "It's been too long. I've missed hanging out with you," he said.

"Yeah, man. For sure."

Teddy pulled out a pill bottle from his pocket and rattled it around. "Want one?"

He wasn't married at the time of this trip, but had just begun dating the girl who would later become his ex-wife and the mother of his child.

"Lortabs?"

Teddy nodded. "You gonna light that joint up?" he said.

"I figured we'd smoke it right before we got to the airport. Have us a little buzz for the flight. I'm good on the tabs though."

Teddy popped one and said, "Let's have a drink."

Rodney grabbed the half-pint of Captain Morgan's Spiced Rum from underneath the passenger seat and unscrewed the cap. He took a swig of the rum followed by a swig of warm soda from a can that sat between them in the car's console. Rodney handed Teddy the rum, and he took a drink of it but didn't bother chasing it with the soda.

"Remember that trip we took to Jacksonville?" Rodney asked.

"It took us what, fifteen hours to make it home?" He smoked a cigarette nearly down to the filter and flung it out the window.

"We couldn't get the son of a bitch over thirty," Rodney said. He took a good drag on his cigarette, filling his lungs full of cancerous smoke, before letting it slowly exhale through his nose.

"Fucking ran that thing back, overheating the whole way home. Stopped every couple of minutes to put some water in her. But she made it."

"We should've just waited till morning and replaced the radiator, huh?"

"Fuck it. I was tired. We were young. We did a lot of surfing those three days, though."

They reminisced about the swell of Hurricane Diana that churned up along the East Coast creating an overhead swell from Sebastian Inlet to Jacksonville Beach. Teddy and Rodney decided school would be there when they got back, but there was a chance to catch an epic swell only so often. When they arrived at Hannah Park to surf the Mayport Poles, it was the best surf either had ever seen. Surfers always claimed it was the best they had ever seen, but that time it really was. After the first day and seven hours of memorable surf, they stayed the night and caught the early morning swell. They rolled out sleeping bags in the bed of the truck, and ended up doing the same thing the next day. On the third day, the swell died and they headed home. Thirty minutes out of the Jacksonville traffic the truck began to run hard. Teddy slept in the passenger side and Rodney was at the wheel when the engine started smoking.

"You were pissed as hell," Rodney said.

"No shit. I didn't know how we'd get home without any money."

"Not one person stopped to ask if we needed any help," Rodney said and then laughed.

"It's funny now," Teddy said and he lit up another cigarette.

Rodney flung his butt out the window and watched a couple girls walk by on the way to the beach and then said, "Just a couple of shirtless, shoeless, long-haired kids stranded on the side of the road with a piece of shit smoking truck with surfboards hanging out the back, hundreds of miles from home with no money and no clue about anything. Just out trying to have as much fun as possible."

Teddy laughed. "Was a damn good time, wasn't it?"

"Wouldn't trade it for nothing."

"I'm glad we're doing it again. Tell the truth, I wasn't so sure we ever would."

"I know I damn sure need it. Fuck it, let's get high."

They lit up the joint and sat smoking while listening to a mixed cd Teddy made specifically for the trip, music from their youth that trapped them in a moment of nostalgia. After a few songs, Teddy started the car and drove to the airport and they finished the bottle of rum just as they entered the airport parking lot.

They checked their boards, the only luggage they carried. Clothes and toiletries were in the board bags, too.

"I could use a beer," Teddy said.

They went to the counter of a deli cart.

"We'll take two beers," Teddy said to the young girl working the counter.

She poured two beers from the tap.

"No. Two each," Teddy said. "We don't wanna have to come back and bother you."

She smiled.

Teddy brought along a deck of cards and sat on the floor flipping over cards as if he were playing blackjack. Rodney sipped his beer and watched Teddy play. Something was different about Teddy, Rodney thought. He didn't seem present anymore, preoccupied with something other than a surf trip. It almost seemed as if he was only going on the trip to fulfill an obligation or maybe to try and recapture a youthfulness that was rapidly slipping from him.

Rodney fell asleep as soon as they got on the plane and woke up as it landed in San Juan. The connecting flight to Aguadilla waited for them on the tarmac and they walked out to the twelve-seat prop-plane. All the luggage was placed under the plane, but their board bags sat on the ground next to the plane. They were told the boards wouldn't fit, but were reassured someone from the airline would deliver them by van first thing in the morning.

"Fuck that," Rodney said. "Find a way to take them now. I was told it would be no problem."

"Yes sir. I understand, but it doesn't fit."

"I need to speak to a manager." Rodney was already speaking to the manager.

"I'm sorry, sir. The other passengers are already loaded and the plane must leave soon."

"Let's just go," Teddy said.

"You're fucking crazy," Rodney told him.

"Sir," the manager said. "Give us the address where you will be staying and we will bring them to you tomorrow morning. You go to sleep tonight and when you wake up, you will have your boards."

"I'm surfing today," Rodney said. "I need my boards with me today."

"It takes three hours by car to get to Aguadilla. We get them to you today, sir. Now please, we are holding everyone up."

"We aren't going to Aquadilla. We are going to Rincón."

"Okay. Rincón then. But sir, really you must board the plane now."

"Let's just go," Teddy said again.

They didn't. They walked back to the terminal to rent a car as the plane they were supposed to catch taxied onto the runway to prepare for takeoff.

The first three rental places told them they must be twenty-five years old to rent a car. They were both only twenty-four. Finally, they found one that said they could rent them one; however, they didn't have any cars available. There were a few in Aguadilla, but it would take three hours to bring it to San Juan. Rodney laughed. Teddy not so much.

"This sucks," Teddy said.

"Just part of the fun of traveling."

"How the fuck is this fun?"

"Just making more stories like Jacksonville."

"Whatever."

The difference was that Teddy never traveled. He wasn't accustomed to the hiccups of exploration. Rodney had been to Europe with some guys from the ball team after his junior year. Mainly just to go to Amsterdam for the cannabis and prostitutes, but they did visit Berlin, too.

Rodney laughed some more. "We could hitchhike?" he said.

"I'm not hitching a ride. I won't hitch a ride in goddamn Brownsville let alone Puerto-fuckin-Rico," Teddy said.

"Let's just ask the next person who rents a car if they could take us. We'll offer them money."

They sat on the floor a few feet from the rental counter. Within five minutes a young lady approached the counter.

"Go ask her." Rodney said.

"I'm not asking. We should have just took the fucking plane."

"And risk not getting our shit back? Just go ask her?"

"I'm not asking. We'll wait for them to bring a car."

Rodney walked over and asked the lady.

"What'd she say?" Teddy asked as Rodney walked back to him.

"Said she had a full car. Her friends were waiting outside."

"She was lying."

"Maybe."

Rodney asked the next person and he was told that he didn't speak English, or he acted like he didn't. Rodney asked five or six people. No one would even consider it.

"I'm walking," Rodney said. "Someone will pick us up."

"I'm not hitching a ride. That's stupid as hell."

"We're two grown-ass men. If anyone picks us up we would be able to beat the shit out of them if they try anything. I'm not waiting here for three hours."

Rodney picked up his bag and headed for the door. Teddy reluctantly followed. They walked for close to an hour in silence and were just about at the on-ramp to the expressway. Rodney led with his thumb out, alternating the board-bag from one arm to the other every couple minutes and Teddy followed about ten feet behind with one hand in his pocket and dragging his board-bag behind him. Every time Rodney looked back and smiled, Teddy gave him the middle finger.

A van slowed down and pulled onto the shoulder. Rodney jogged up to the driver's window. A fat man with a mustache and tropical shirt half unbuttoned said he was heading to Mayaguez, and Rincón was on the way.

"Told you it would be fine," Rodney said.

"Shut up," Teddy said.

Rodney climbed in the passenger seat and Teddy sat in the back. The man had some rope in the back and tied the board bags to the roof.

"You think he carries rope around for tying up hitchhikers?" Rodney whispered to Teddy.

He gave Rodney the finger again.

The fat man was from Puerto Rico and lived in New York now. He was back to visit his elderly mom. He came back three or four times a year. He told them his name, but neither Teddy nor Rodney really listened.

"What do you know about Rincón?" Rodney asked.

"Not much out there. Why did you decide to go there?"

"To surf Tres Palmas."

"Have any other plans while here? Visit San Juan? Anything?"

"No. Just wanted to hang out and get some good surf for about ten days. That's pretty much it. Thought about going to that bioluminescent bay, but heard you need a full moon to really see it."

"Surf only. No women?"

"Women would be cool, too. Why not?"

Fat Man said he was going to visit a place in Isabela.

"Plenty of women," Fat Man said.

Teddy didn't look too keen on the idea.

Around the city of Bajadero, Fat Man asked if they were hungry. He stopped at a Church's Chicken and ordered a bucket of thighs and legs and didn't ask for any money in return. Rodney grabbed a drumstick and handed one back to Teddy. Teddy didn't smile. Rodney did. Teddy shook his head and snatched the chicken from his hand.

"Relax. It'll be all right," Rodney said. Teddy bit into his chicken and looked out the window.

"Your friend okay?" Fat Man asked. He looked at Teddy through the rearview mirror.

"Yeah. I guess he's a bit nervous, hitchhiking and all."

"You think I might try to do something to you?" Fat Man asked Teddy.

Teddy shook his head. "No. Just tired."

"You don't want to stop and see women? It's fine. I drop you guys off first."

"No," Rodney said. "He wants to go."

"You want to go?" Fat Man said through a mouth full of chicken and small dribble of grease on his chin.

"Whatever," Teddy said. "Yeah. Fine. I'll go."

"Ahh. Your friend wants women," Fat Man said and nudged him with a drumstick bone before he tossed it from the window.

They drove around a residential area of Isabela and then pulled into a parking lot bordered on one side by a wooded area.

"This is a great town. Beautiful beaches. Beautiful women. We call it the City of Fighting Cocks," Fat Man said.

"We can cock fight here?" Rodney asked.

"Sure."

"No shit? Legally?"

"Yes, legally. We have an arena and everything. You want to go?"

"Hell yea, I want to go."

"Okay. Tomorrow they fight. Only on Sundays. I pick you up and we go."

"I can get down with some cockfights," Teddy said.

"Goddamn, right."

They exited the car and placed the boards inside the van. They walked past the wooded area and came to a strip mall.

"It's just out in the open like this?" Rodney asked.

"Sure. It's just a massage," Fat Man said and winked.

"Looks sketchy," Teddy said.

"You don't have to go," Fat Man told him. "Are you married?"

"No, he's not," Rodney said.

"I have a fiancé," Teddy said.

"Then it's okay," Fat Man told him.

"See. It's okay," Rodney said with a huge smile.

Teddy managed a smirk.

"Yeah, man," Rodney said and gave Teddy a one-armed side-hug. "That's it. Loosen up. We're here to have fun."

"I could just get a massage if I wanted. Not like I'm required to fuck, right?"

"Whatever you want," Rodney said.

"I know what I'm doing," Fat Man said.

"I bet you do," Rodney said. He turned to Teddy, "You forgot how much fun trouble is, didn't you?"

"Yeah, I haven't really done much lately. Just busting my ass at work."

"Well, we're letting loose these ten days."

Fat Man knocked on one of the doors. There weren't any signs or anything, just a blackout door with the word *Mandy's* stenciled on it, and a man cracked the door and said something in Spanish. Fat Man spoke to him in a whisper and then the door opened wider and allowed all three of them in. The place was dark with purple carpeted walls and there was only a counter and a cash register.

Prices were seventy dollars for forty-five minutes.

"I don't have that kind of cash," Rodney said.

"I got it," Fat Man said. "I take care of my guests."

Fat Man spoke with the man again and paid him some undisclosed amount and then led Rodney and Teddy to another room. Eight girls stood in thongs and bras. Two girls quickly took off their bras and perked up their nipples with a quick pinch.

There were four love seats arranged in a square and a coffee table in the middle. The room smelled heavy of lavender, cinnamon, and cigars.

"Have a seat," Fat Man said. "We'll have some fun for a bit and then when you are ready, pick your girl. She'll lead the way."

Teddy and Rodney sat next to each other on a love seat, and two girls quickly sat on their laps. The one that sat on Rodney's lap looked about nineteen in the body but about forty-six in the face. The one on Teddy's lap looked forty-six all the way around. Fat Man sat down with three girls, and the other girls sat on the empty love seat. Those girls looked young, but maybe they were the rookies and weren't allowed to be as aggressive as the veterans. Rodney wanted one of them.

Rodney rubbed the brown leg on his lap and Teddy looked ahead, hands by his side, as his girl ran her fingers through his hair.

"Thinking about what to tell Alexa when she asks how Puerto Rico was?" Rodney asked him.

Teddy flipped him a bird.

Fat Man then plopped a mound of cocaine on the coffee table. The man who had opened the door for them came in the room with a bottle of rum and a tray of cups filled with ice and set it on the table. One of the young girls poured everyone drinks.

"I don't have many people to party with when I come down here, so it was good running into you guys," Fat Man said. "You seem like alright guys."

"We appreciate your hospitality," Rodney said. "Whatcha think?" he asked Teddy.

Teddy nodded and took a sip of his rum and then lifted the woman off his leg and kneeled by the table to cut himself a rail of cocaine. The girl did one with him. Rodney did one next, and then for the next hour or so, they snorted and drank until Fat Man said it was time for him to go in the back. His girl led him to another room and two others followed.

"Damn. Dude is taking three girls back there," Teddy said.

"He's done this before," Rodney said.

"Are you ready?" the lady hanging on Rodney asked.

Rodney looked at Teddy and asked, "You going back now?"

"Might have another drink," he said.

"I'll have one with you." Then Rodney asked the lady, "Can I take two of you back?"

"You want two girls?" she asked.

"I do."

"Yeah, if I'm going back there, I guess I want two, too," Teddy said.

"Okay," she said. "You have two girls."

Teddy and Rodney smiled at each other and then bent their faces to the table and snorted another line as long and as thick as their pinky fingers.

They sat back on the love seat, and Rodney's girl straddled him and took off her bra, hanging her breasts into his face. Teddy's girl sat on his lap with her back to him, gyrating to faint music that neither of the Americans had noticed until that moment.

Another girl ran through the door and said something in

Spanish. She sounded panicked. Neither Rodney nor Teddy spoke Spanish, but both understood *policia*.

The women jumped up quickly and led them by the hand and directed them into a hatch in the hallway. They could only fit through on their hands and knees. Rodney went in first and Teddy was close behind. The girls shut the hatch behind them. There was a string of Christmas lights lining the top and it led down a narrow passage. They continued on through twists and turns, neither speaking. Their heavy breathing was the only sound.

It led to a screen opening and Rodney punched through and scrambled out, falling about six feet to the wet ground. Teddy tumbled on top of him. There were two similar holes coming out of the building's side.

"That fat dude can't fit through that passage."

"Jesus Christ," Teddy said. "I swear to God if I go to a Puerto Rican jail I will fucking kill you."

Teddy ran through the woods. Rodney followed him through thickets and briers and came to an opening at the edge of the parking lot. The van was there with only a few other cars.

"Let's just go somewhere," Teddy said. "Ask the next person we see where the closest hotel is and go the fuck home tomorrow."

"Fuck that. We came to surf. I ain't going back after one day."

"How're we gonna get our boards?" Teddy said and looked through the window of the van. "Jesus. I can't believe I let you talk me into going to a place like that."

Rodney ignored the last part and said, "We can bust a window." Rodney looked around the parking lot for a rock. Before finding one, he heard a loud thud and Teddy shouted out a string of profanities.

"What the fuck did you do?" Rodney said, rushing up to him.

Teddy was bent double holding his hand between his thighs.

"Holy shit! Did you try to punch out a window? How fucked up are you?"

"Pretty fucking fucked up," Teddy said through clenched teeth. "So fucked up, I just tried to punch out a van window, asshole."

"Don't get pissed at me."

"It's your fault we're in this shit."

"Fuck you. I was just trying to have some fun."

"We were on a trip to Puerto Rico. Isn't that fun enough?"

Rodney found a rock and slammed it through the back window. He took off his shirt, wrapped it around his hand, and broke away the shards that surrounded the window. When it was cleared of glass he pulled the boards through the opened back window.

They walked down the street and after a few minutes watched four police cars drive past. A fat man looked to be in the back seat of the last police car.

Thirty minutes of walking and they came upon the beach.

"Let's just sleep on the beach for tonight," Rodney said.

"I think my hand is really fucked up."

"It hurts?"

"Yeah, it hurts."

"Eat another lortab."

"I already popped three."

"Rum, cocaine, and three lortabs? You should be feeling pretty good. Give me one."

"Fuck you."

They sat on the beach and Rodney gathered some wood and built a fire that they lay next to until sleep overcame them. Sleep happened upon Rodney rather effortlessly. Not so much for Teddy.

Rodney woke up to a blazing sun and the sound of waves crashing just offshore. Teddy was smoking a cigarette. He said he didn't sleep the whole night.

"Holy shit, man. Look at that. Head high at least." Rodney pointed to the perfect a-frame barrels peeling just off shore.

"Look at my hand," Teddy said. It was swollen and turning three different shades of blue.

"Does it hurt?"

"Like a motherfucker."

"Can you surf?"

"My hand is broke."

"You don't know that."

"I'm pretty damn sure."

"What do you wanna do?"

"Go to a hospital."

Rodney stepped out and waved down a cab. The cab couldn't take the boards so the cab-driver said he could call for a van cab, but there was no telling how long that would take. Rodney convinced Teddy to go on and that he would stay back to watch their stuff.

As soon as the cab drove off, Rodney went straight for the water. He surfed a good three hours of perfect head-high waves. When Rodney finally came in, Teddy was waiting for him where the board bags were.

"You just left our shit lying around?"

"Everything's there, right?"

"Yeah. But it might not have been."

"But it is. What's up with your hand?"

Teddy lifted it up. It was wrapped in a bandage and his pinky was secured with a tongue depressor.

"A fucking tongue depressor?" Rodney said.

Teddy nodded. Rodney laughed and without thinking, even pointed.

"What'd the doctor say?"

"It's broke. Said I need surgery. He could've done it, but fuck that, I'm going home."

"He charge you anything?"

"No."

"Damn dude. Should have gotten a free surgery then."

"You're an idiot."

"What a trip, huh? Only one day. At least I caught some pretty good surf."

"I saw that one you got barreled on. Looked nice."

A van finally came and took them to Aguadilla where they were put on the next flight out.

Teddy went back to heating and air and Rodney went

back to pursuing baseball. He was offered a contract to play in the Rookie League. He accepted, but was already one of the older guys on the team at twenty-five. He played for three years and made it up to Low A, but then was sent back down and at twenty-eight, realized his chance had pretty much slipped away. He was only making about twelve hundred a month, about half as much as what he was making as a teacher. He decided to hang up his cleats and focus on a career. He got hired on at the University of Miami as an athletic trainer for the baseball team. It wasn't "the Show," but he gave it a good run. Now, at thirty-three years old, that Puerto Rico trip seemed like a lifetime ago.

* * * *

"We always said we'd go back some day and do it right," Teddy said.

"I know, man. Who knows? We still might some time."

"Yeah, we might."

"It was still kind of fun though, huh? I know it sounds like bullshit, but it was worth it to me."

"Wish I could've surfed."

"It wasn't worth it to you?"

Teddy chuckled. "It was."

They sipped their beers.

"So you're heading back to Miami tomorrow, huh?"

"Yep."

Teddy nodded.

"Little Anthony doing all right?"

Teddy nodded again. "He's good. Likes baseball. Already a Cubs fan."

"Poor kid," Rodney said.

"He really is a great kid."

"Good, man. Good."

"Well, I'm going to take off," Teddy said. "Thanks for the laughs."

Rodney watched as Teddy walked off. He didn't have the heart to tell Teddy that he had been back to Puerto Rico. A few times. For some reason, he felt that Teddy needed a trip to look forward to, even if he knew he would never make it.

The Defeated

Hank Ackerman continued staining the Philippine mahogany of the canoe he built in shop class while listening to the conversation of the other boys who were supposed to be helping him. Hank wore a shower cap to keep the long strands of his hair from getting caught in the belt sander. The other three boys—Milt Andrews, Raymond Ragsdale, and Cole Peoples—all had short, buzzed hair. Milt's was nearly to the scalp. They all wore dirty aprons and smudged goggles.

Milt was a junior starting linebacker on the varsity squad. He was a hunter and talked about that the most, until recently when he started talking about boxing, which he and the other two did nearly every day after school now that football season was over. They boxed at Milt's uncle's barn. From what Hank heard, Milt was the boxing champ of Sullivan High School.

Raymond, the tall, lanky, uncoordinated-looking kid, was a senior second-string defensive back. When Raymond talked about who he had beaten up last, Hank couldn't help but think he was full of shit. Hank knew he could take Raymond. Milt, he wasn't so sure. But definitely Raymond and without a doubt, Cole. But he wouldn't ever want to fight Cole. He would be embarrassed if for some reason he lost. Cole was short, 5' 6" tops, but with shoulders that made him look like an inverted triangle. He bench-pressed nearly three hundred pounds and was the senior second-string running back and starting defensive back. No one put as much heart into football practice as Cole did. He was definitely a shoe-in for Homecoming King this year, too.

Hank knew some of Cole's opponents and was surprised to hear he fought them, and even more surprised to hear he won a few. But even when he lost, Milt always commented on what a good show Cole put on. Even with all the talk, Hank was convinced he could beat Cole.

"Hank, why don't you come box with us?" Milt said. This was not the first time he asked him and normally Hank ignored him. But he was tired of hearing how tough they were. He was tired of the bragging and how everyone looked up to Milt. Milt was the best football player, now the boxing champ, and all the girls said he had the biggest cock.

"Who would I fight?" Hank asked.

"I'll fight you." Raymond said.

"Yeah, fight Raymond," Milt said. "That'll be a good start."

"If you beat him, you can fight me," Cole said.

"What's that supposed to mean?" Raymond asked.

"That I can kick your ass," Cole said.

Milt laughed. "It's true."

"He didn't kick my ass. It was a draw," Raymond said. "You even said so."

"I was being nice. He kicked your ass," Milt said and laughed some more.

"I hit you harder than my balls slapping on Jenny's ass," Cole said. Milt and Raymond found that funny. Hank shook his head. He couldn't understand what girls saw in these guys.

The bell rang and they took off their aprons and goggles. Hank took off his shower cap, and all four left class together.

When they got outside, they split ways.

"Swing by today, if you wanna fight," Milt said.

"All right," Hank said.

During the ten minutes between classes, Milt, Raymond, and Cole hung out with the cheerleaders and other jocks and it wasn't really known that they talked to people like Hank except in shop class. Hank had his own group that he associated with and he didn't want them to think that he was acquainted with people like those three either. Hank mainly hung out with Charles Gutterman, the only other surfer at school. They also hung out with the few stoners at the school, the long-hairs who wore Pink Floyd shirts and hung out at the pool hall. People thought it was crazy that Hank and Charlie would waste an hour or more to drive to Pensacola Beach for only a couple hours of surf. For Hank and Charlie, it was more than worth it. Even if the waves were only knee-high and too small to surf, they would drive out there just to get in the water and paddle around. Hank's surfboard was a hand-me-down from his brother Teddy, and to Hank, surfing seemed like such an alien world from what he had grown up in, and Pensacola Beach was as close to another world as he could get.

He found Charlie behind the stadium sharing a joint with a few other kids. Under the stadium smoking a joint was about the only place you would see black and white kids hanging out together at Sullivan High, except football practice, but that didn't count.

"What's up, Hank. Wanna hit this?" Jeremy asked. Jeremy was a long-hair who looked like a rat, small and sleazy with greasy hair. At least Hank kept his hair washed on a regular basis and pulled back in a ponytail. Jeremy had strands that hung down in his eyes, and there was something about him that Hank never liked. He never trusted him, but he was who Charlie usually got his pot from.

Hank shook Charlie's hand and nobody else's. They only received a nod. Charlie wore long hair at one time, too, but he said he didn't like how it got tangled when he went surfing, so he buzzed it short.

"I gotta get to class," Brigit said and handed the joint to Hank. "One more tardy and Mrs. P'll give me a detention." She would sit in science class and comb her red hair for what seemed like hours. It wasn't her real color and if she wasn't combing her hair, she sometimes made a list of all the boys she fucked. There were more boys than birthdays. Hank felt ashamed every time he saw his name near the end of the list. Jeremy, Charlie, even Milt and Raymond, were ahead of him. He slept with her for the first time two months ago after a year of saying he never would.

Jeremy then left and the two black boys did, too.

"You guys want to hit this?" Charlie asked the two kids that were playing hacky-sack.

"We're good, man," one said.

"Just you and me," Charlie said. They finished the joint and walked slowly to class, late and squinty-eyed. Hank had tenth-grade English next. He hated walking into a class of younger kids. He couldn't believe he failed that class last year. He may not have read more books than the teacher, but he was pretty sure the books he read were better. He thought that because the teacher never read Bukowski, Ginsberg, or Burroughs and never even heard of Harry Crews, Larry Brown, or Barry Hannah, books Hank borrowed from Teddy's friend Rodney. Rodney told him, "If you are going to read, you might as well read something worth a shit."

"Nice of you to join us," Mr. Moore said as Hank entered. The kids laughed. It didn't bother him when most of the kids laughed. They were idiots anyway, he thought. But Jenny was different. She shouldn't have laughed. Hank still couldn't figure out what she saw in Cole.

"We are going over the quizzes, but I'm sure you already know what you got," Mr. Moore said.

Hank didn't realize he was still staring at Jenny's angelic face. She smiled. The other kids laughed again.

"I'm going to the restroom," Hank said.

"Please do," Mr. Moore said. Mr. Moore allowed Hank to do anything as long as it meant he would be out of the class and unable to disrupt the other students.

He caught Jenny's eye again before he left, and she stopped smiling. She looked disappointed. He shrugged his shoulders and walked out.

He walked out to Charlie's car and waited until the final bell rang.

"Just called the report. Head-high," Charlie said when school ended.

They drove home and got their surfboards and rolled a joint on the way to the beach.

"You think I could beat Milt?" Hank asked passing the lit joint to Charlie. Charlie inserted a tape into the tape deck with one hand while guiding the wheel with his knee as he reached across, grabbing the joint with his other hand.

"Whatya mean beat him? In a fight?"

"Yeah, boxing."

"Don't tell me you're thinking of going over there."

"I'm telling you, I think Jenny likes me. You oughta see the looks she gives me. If I beat the hell outta the so-called champ, then she's gonna like me even more. And you oughta hear the way that dickhead, Cole, talks about her. It's sick, man. She's too good, you know, too pretty to be hanging out with jackasses like that."

"Then why not just beat Cole?"

"Cause I want to beat the champ."

"Since when do you give a shit about what those assholes at school think, anyway?"

"I don't care about them."

"Jesus, man. You sound like a fucking schoolboy movie. It's not for them, it's for her. You should hear yourself."

"Whatever. Are we going?"

"Where?"

"To the barn."

"No. I'm going surfing."

"Drop me off then."

"Shut up. We're going surfing. Smoke this and mellow out."

"I'm serious. Drop me off." Hank put the joint out in the ashtray.

"What're you doing? I was smoking that."

"Drop me off."

"Jesus Christ." Charlie turned the car around. "This better be worth missing waves for," he said.

"Thanks," Hank said. He lit the joint back up and gave it to Charlie.

There was a crowd outside of the barn. Hank's last time at the barn was nearly ten years ago, the day Shithead died. He knew Milt was Lenny Jr.'s nephew and that made him want to fight Milt even more.

It wasn't just the kids from school there either. Lenny Jr. stood off to the side with a few of his friends, betting on the fights.

"I didn't know this many people came," Hank said.

"We can turn around."

"For what?" Hank said.

"I don't know. I don't want to be here anymore than you do."

There were at least twenty people making a human ring. It was the place Milt pummeled other saps who wanted to prove something. Jenny was there. She stood away from the crowd, talking with one of her girlfriends.

Charlie pulled the car into the lot across the street.

"Look, she ain't even interested in this bullshit," Charlie said. "You're gonna look foolish. She doesn't care who you can beat."

Hank walked straight ahead. He didn't push his way into the crowd to watch Milt pound the other guy, but by the sound of the moans and oohs and aahs of the crowd, Hank knew it was bad. Charlie waited by the car.

Jenny saw Hank and left her girlfriend to talk to him.

"What're you doing here?" she asked.

"I came to…uhm…" Hank looked into her soft eyes, pale, smooth face, and the faint freckles on her nose. He wished he could kiss her, but he was beginning to realize how stupid it was that he was there. Charlie was right. She didn't care who he could beat.

"Hey you made it, huh?" Cole said, walking up and smacking Jenny on her ass. "Get me a drink, will ya, babe." She turned and walked off as Hank watched her, and Cole watched Hank watching her.

"That's my girlfriend you're staring at, asshole."

"What?"

"She sure is pretty, ain't she?" Cole said.

Hank only nodded.

"So who you want? Who do you want to fight?" Cole said.

Hank looked at Cole. "Milt. I want to fight Milt."

Cole laughed. The crowd cheered loudly as Milt's opponent made his way out of the circle, his nose bloody and left eye puffed.

"Wait here. Wait till Milt hears this." Cole ran over to Milt.

Milt came over as the crowd mingled, waiting for the next beating. "You gotta earn your right to challenge me. Make your way through the ranks."

"I'm ready," Hank said, straight-faced.

"At least fight Cole here," Milt said.

Hank shook his head. Jenny came out with a light beer for Cole and one for Hank. Hank smiled as she handed it to him. His hand grazed hers and he thought she held her hand there for a moment to prolong the touch.

"I'll talk to Lenny Jr. Let him know we are just going to spar," Milt said, and he put a pinch of spit-tobacco in his lip.

"I don't want to spar. I want to beat you."

"You've lost your damn mind, Hank," Milt said.

"I don't care. I want to go for real."

"Okay. We'll go for real. Give me ten minutes." He spit a black glob that landed close to Hank's shoe. Milt smiled and a little dribble of tobacco hung off his chin. He wiped it away with the back of his hand. "Give me ten minutes and we'll fight," he said and walked off.

Cole led Jenny away, and she turned and said, "Good luck."

Hank went back across the street. "I'm next. You want this?" He handed the beer to Charlie who downed it in two gulps.

"You can't lose," Charlie said. "This is your shot. You gotta do whatever you can, but don't lose, asshole. This isn't just for you or for her; it's for every kid who those assholes make fun of. This is for every kid who was ever given a wedgy. Every kid who ever got their gym clothes shit and pissed on. You are the peon rising against the kingdom."

"Shut up," Hank said cutting him off.

Charlie laughed. "Just trying to make it somewhat entertaining," he said. "You realize how stupid this is, right?"

Cole laced up Hank's gloves. "He's gonna kick the shit

out of you," Cole said and laughed. "And you know damn well you never stood a chance with Jenny."

Raymond tied up Milt's gloves.

Hank couldn't hear the crowd's murmur. He couldn't hear anything except his heart beat. It sounded as if it were trying to escape his body through his ears. Charlie slapped him on the back of the neck.

"Nervous?"

Hank nodded and said, "I shouldn't have gotten high."

Charlie laughed. "Not many people betting on ya."

"I figured. What did you bet?"

"I'm not a betting man," Charlie said.

"But if you were."

"I'll tell you after the fight."

Raymond and Milt walked to the center.

"Let's go," Cole said.

Hank hesitated. He looked around at the crowd. He could see the excitement in everyone's eyes. He could sense their thirst for blood. He found who he was looking for. She smiled and lifted a hand in a sly attempt at a wave. He met Milt at the center.

"You know the rules, right?" Raymond said.

Hank nodded. Milt smiled, not looking like he was ready for a fight. Hank didn't look up at Milt's eyes, but focused on the mocking smile with the tobacco pushing out the lower lip.

"Just no hitting below the belt," Cole said. "I'll keep time. Two minute rounds. Two minute rests. Raymond'll be the ref. Ready?"

Hank nodded. Milt stuck out his gloves. Hank tapped them.

"You're supposed to hit 'em," Milt said and slammed his gloves down on top of Hank's gloves with force. "It's just for fun, man. Lighten up," Milt said. "No one expects you to actually win."

Cole and Raymond laughed. Raymond motioned them to start.

Hank put his gloves in front of his face. Milt hunched over in a crab-like stance and threw two quick left jabs, not hard, just measuring distance. Hank kept looking at the smile. Milt did a silly dance and threw a couple more distance-measuring left jabs and then came with a right hook that caught Hank in the ear. The crowd laughed. Milt backed up and bounced around a little on his toes imitating Roy Jones, Jr. imitating Muhammad Ali. Hank shook his head and marched forward. Milt backed him up with a couple of more jabs. He then backed off again, still smiling.

"You okay?" Milt said to him.

Hank responded by lurching after him again with two quick jabs and then came with a wild haymaker that caught Milt unexpectedly. The crowd gasped. Hank was shocked by the punch. He didn't think it was going to land. Milt stumbled and regained his footing.

"So we're really boxing, huh?" Milt said. He spit out his wad of tobacco and said, "I was just fucking with you, but now you're gonna get it. I'm gonna fuck you up."

Hank didn't answer. He just looked at the smile. Milt came forward. A quick three-punch combo put Hank on the ground. Hank blocked the first left jab, but the straight right that followed was too quick, and he didn't even feel or see the left hook that laid him out. He lifted to a seated position and struggled to focus. He saw Charlie shake his head in disappointment. He saw Jenny cover her mouth in fear. Cole bent beside him as Raymond continued counting, "…Three…four…five…"

"You wanna call it?" Cole asked.

Hank stood up. He shook his head.

"He wants more," Cole yelled.

Milt waited back and waved him in with his gloves, still smiling and dancing. Hank shuffled forward, his eyes trying to focus on one of the two Milts. When he got in close range, he began swinging wildly, punch after punch. Milt did, too. Neither one was boxing anymore. It became a fight. Milt wrapped his arms around Hank's torso and tackled him like they were on the football field. Hank elbowed Milt in the mouth that wasn't smiling anymore. Raymond and Cole separated them before it went too far. As they pulled Milt back, blood trickled from his lip.

"You're fucking dead," Milt said.

During the two-minute rest, Raymond walked over to Hank and Cole.

"Milt wants to know if it's over. You busted his mouth," he said.

Hank shook his head.

"He doesn't want it to turn into a street fight," Raymond said. "He wants to box. But you're starting to piss him off."

"Milt's the one who tackled him," Charlie shouted and

pushed his way to Hank. Jenny followed.

"He thought Hank was pissed. He didn't know if they were boxing anymore. He thought it was serious," Raymond said.

"Of course it was fucking serious," Jenny said. "They're fighting."

Hank turned to look at her.

"You gonna stop?" Cole asked.

Hank looked at Charlie. Charlie shrugged his shoulders. "Up to you, man."

Hank peered around Raymond and saw Milt bouncing around shadow boxing and punching himself in the head. He knew there was no way to win this. He looked at Jenny.

"He's not stopping," Jenny said.

Cole looked at her. Hank smiled. Raymond went over to tell Milt the fight was on.

"You're going out there and kicking Milt's ass," she said.

"Why the fuck are you cheering for him?" Cole said.

Raymond motioned them back into the center. The crowd hushed. Hank started walking out to the center and Jenny grabbed him by the arm. She gave him a quick peck on the cheek. "Good luck," she said.

Hank looked at Cole for an expression. Cole glared at Hank. Hank winked at him and Cole lurched at Hank, but Jenny grabbed him by the arm to stop him, and Hank walked off while Jenny and Cole shouted at each other.

Hank and Milt touched gloves again. Milt smiled. His teeth a little pink this time. This gave Hank a boost of confidence.

"No elbows this time, pussy," Milt said.

"Then don't tackle me," Hank said.

"Got a little carried away." Milt smiled.

The crowd grew silent again. Hank tried to put together a plan, but before he could put together a thought Milt charged forward and an overhand right landed on Hank's chin with a left uppercut to his stomach directly behind it that felt as if it penetrated his gut, severed his spine, and came out his back. Hank dropped to his knees and then leaned over onto his forehead, gasping for air.

Jenny came to his aid and told him to stand up with his hands over his head to catch his breath. Instead he fell over onto his side and gasped like a fish plucked from an aquarium. Cole left the crowd and retreated out of sight.

"I'm stopping it," Jenny said.

Hank didn't hear her. She stood up. Charlie ran to her and said, "You aren't stopping shit." Milt and Raymond were now standing over him. Raymond counting.

"Four...Five..."

"Get up," Charlie said. "Get the fuck the up." He lifted Hank by the arms. Jenny fell back into the inner edge of the crowd, biting her nails.

"Stop counting," Charlie said. "He's all right."

"Seven...Eight..." Raymond said.

"I said stop counting, you fuckface," Charlie said, grabbing Raymond by the collar and shaking him until he stopped counting and then he threw Raymond to the ground.

"It's over," Milt said showing his pink teeth.

"The fuck it is," Charlie said. Hank was bent over clutching his ribs, but his breathing was returning to normal.

"You probably broke a rib," Raymond said as he stood from the ground and cowered behind Milt. He and Milt laughed.

"Can't hang with the big boys, huh?" Milt said. "Should stick to surfing and hacky-sack, you faggots."

Charlie helped Hank up. "He's all right," he said. "Say you're all right."

Hank didn't say it.

"Goddamn it, Hank. Say you are all right."

Hank straightened up. "I'm all right," he said. "Let's go."

"You really want more? I'll fucking kill you."

"I'm ready."

"If that's what you want."

Charlie whispered something into Hank's ear and went back, standing at Jenny's side.

"What did you tell him?" she asked.

"Just some words of encouragement."

Hank and Milt touched gloves in the center and began again. Hank crouched lower this time, trying to protect his gut. Milt dropped his hands to his side. "I'll even…"

Before Milt could finish his sentence, Hank sprung up and hit him with a solid right hook that rocked Milt backwards, but he recovered quickly enough and Hank was back on the defensive.

Milt came at him full force and threw a flurry of punches that knocked Hank over. Hank was covered well and it wasn't the punches that sent him down. He was trying to back-pedal and tripped. Milt backed up, allowing Hank to get to his feet. Hank looked at Jenny and Charlie and knew what he had to do.

He took a deep breath that stung under his ribs and walked forward. Milt stood his ground. Hank threw an uppercut with all the force that was left in him. It was going to be his final punch. He would have nothing left in him afterward. It landed below the belt sending a pain from Milt's testicles up to his stomach, dropping him to his knees and with his forehead to the ground. He dry-heaved before spewing beer-vomit onto the ground, splattering his legs and chest. The crowd was a loud mix of laughter and booing.

Hank looked at Charlie and grinned. Charlie returned it with a half-grin of his own. Hank then looked at Jenny and shrugged his shoulders. She smiled, too.

Hank and Raymond stood over Milt.

"You asshole," Raymond said to Hank. "There's no hitting below the belt."

"It was an accident," Hank told him. "I got a little carried away."

"He's gonna want a rematch. And he's gonna fucking slaughter you."

"It was an accident."

Cole walked to the center of the ring. He looked at Jenny as she hugged Hank, a smile across her face. Instead of going over to her, Cole bent down to help Milt to his feet.

"We still got time to catch some evening surf?" Charlie said.

"I'll go, but I don't think I'll be able to get in the water," Hank said. "You want to come along?" he asked Jenny. "You ever surf before?"

She looked back at Cole. He was helping Raymond hold up Milt, and they were walking him around.

"I would love to," she said. "But I better not. Cole would be so pissed if I did."

Hank nodded. "Yeah he would. Maybe next time?"

"Next time," she said and turned to look for Cole. She turned back around to give Hank a hug goodbye, but he was already walking to the car.

There never was a next time. There never was a rematch either as Hank always rejected the offer, but that didn't stop Milt from getting his revenge one day as Hank ate lunch in the school cafeteria. Hank was okay with that because, as it stood, he was still the only person to ever bring the champ, Milt Andrews, to his knees and no one could ever take that away from him.

White Tropic Dreams

The line at the deli inside the Pensacola Regional Airport continued to grow as Charlie Gutterson sat on the countertop sipping a soda and daydreaming about a life different from the one he lived. He once read that two acres of land in Costa Rica could be purchased for as little as seven-thousand dollars. He knew if he were ever going to have a chance of owning land like that, it was something that had to be done quickly and the minimum-wage job at the airport wasn't cutting it.

"Hey," a man shouted at him, "can I get a bagel? My plane is leaving."

With a smirk, Charlie looked up at the line of people, unaware who had spoken and said, "You better go catch it then, huh?"

"What?" the man shouted back. "Your manager is going to hear about this."

"I am the manager," Charlie said. He was not the manager.

Four months ago, the day after his eighteenth birthday and the day his grandmother died, he moved down to Pensacola to live with his mother and started working at the deli. He thought it would be a good way to network with those who worked for the airlines. He wanted to get a job as a baggage handler. He heard if you worked for an airline, you received free or discounted flights, and his plan was to get a job and go AWOL in Central America. He even ordered himself a passport, but so far, he had not been able to get an interview.

After all the planes took off or landed and the airport was empty except for a few janitors and workaholic ticket agents, he poured himself a pint of Guinness to accompany him while he closed the store. He was washing dishes when he heard the shout from the front of the deli.

"Hey, asshole, open up." It was Vick with a nice surprise and maybe a way for Charlie to finally escape.

* * * *

In Shalimar, Florida, about forty minutes from Pensacola, nestled among large hundred-year-old live oaks overlooking Choctawatchee Bay, sat a two-story Creole-cottage-style house on three acres of land with a spacious two-car garage and a screened-in pool. Eglin Air Force Base was nearby, and jets could often be heard flying overhead. Katelin watched something other than music videos on *MTV* and cursed the location of the house every time she adjusted the volume. She heard her parents' car pull up into the driveway and the garage door open. Her parents were returning from a five-day cruise to the Bahamas, and Katelin went to her room so she wouldn't have to listen to them talk about their vacation.

She was seventeen years old and five months away from graduation. It was the first time they trusted her to stay alone while they went out of town, and she threw only one party. Just a few friends drinking beer, a few people smoked pot, and there was a late-night skinny dip in the pool, but nothing too outrageous for a group of high school seniors. She even kept the door to her parents' bedroom shut throughout the party with a sign written in black sharpie that said, "Keep

Out."

Katelin knew everyone at the party except for three guys — Dustin, Vick, and Charlie. Vick, five-foot-seven with an acne-cratered face, heard from a friend about the get-together and went to sell cocaine. The other two went along for the ride and the free cocaine. Katelin and Vick spent most of the evening talking. As the crowd dispersed, the guys hung around and all three ended up staying the night. Dustin tried to get into the bedroom with Vick and Katelin, but she said she wasn't like that.

Dustin was the shortest of the three. He thought of himself as a ladies' man, but his over-sized ears, undersized chin, and bowed legs were somewhat of a turn-off for most girls.

Dustin fell asleep on the couch the moment his head hit the pillow while Charlie wandered the house, looking at family pictures in the living room and the hallway and then opened up the door with the sign that said, "Keep Out."

The bedroom was spacious, and the bathroom was probably three times the size of the one at his house. The tub, a four-seater with high powered water jets, was separate from the shower, something he never saw before. He ran the water, and after a few minutes, tried adjusting the jets. It took him a few minutes more to figure it out.

He disrobed and stepped into the steaming bath. He laid his head back. The paintings on the walls were all originals, not the cheap hotel reprints he was used to seeing at his mom's house. He stared longest at the one with a shirtless old man sitting in a lopsided, weather-beaten row boat not far off shore. The boat looked like it was either taking on water or was loaded down with enough fish to last a month. The line was taut, but the pole wasn't bent over like in most fishing pictures. The sun was barely breaking over the horizon. Charlie could tell it was going to be a scorcher. Large unfocused palm leaves hung from the right corner, the trunks out of view.

When his eyelids became heavy he exited the tub, leaving a puddle under his feet. He dried off with a towel hanging nearby and stopped in front of the vanity mirror to flex before walking back into the bedroom and settling into the king-sized waterbed. Naked.

The next morning, he awoke to Katelin yelling at Vick about his friend sleeping naked in her parents' room. Dustin's high-pitched laugh penetrated the walls. Charlie pulled on the same pair of jeans he wore for the last six days and the Jim Morrison t-shirt he wore for the last three and walked into the living room.

"I shit in their toilet, too," Charlie said rubbing sleep from his eyes. Dustin laughed. Vick wanted to, but he smiled and nodded his head to let Charlie know he thought it was funny. Katelin shook her head in disgust and slammed the door on her way out.

"Where's she going?" Charlie asked as he opened the refrigerator.

"Said she couldn't wait for our slow asses. Had to go to work or something."

"How many eggs you guys want?" Charlie asked, slapping a tablespoon of butter onto a skillet that was sitting on the stove.

Katelin's parents were only home from their vacation twenty minutes when her father stormed through her bedroom door saying, "We've got a problem."

Katelin noticed for the first time the deep-seated wrinkles around her father's eyes. Her mother stood behind him in the doorway with a concerned look on her face.

* * * *

Police officer Buddy Herring was sitting at his desk as the soon-to-be new investigator of the Shalimar police force. He was working the night shift and reading the *New York Post* on his desk-top. He was a little overweight. Some of the other officers teased him that his pink, balding head resembled the belly of a piglet. They also teased him about his name, not believing him that Buddy was his real name and not a nickname.

Shalimar was a lonely town, a couple of hours west of the popular Spring Break destination, Panama City Beach. That's where the excitement was. Either there or a little farther west in Pensacola, he thought. After thirteen years as a Shalimar police officer, Buddy was patiently awaiting the promotion to detective. He wanted to work on cases that took determination and dedication, the kind of cases that only the most hardboiled detectives could solve. He wanted adventures like the homicide division of New York City that his uncle used to tell him about.

When Buddy was nine, he told his dad, a USMC ace from WWII, he was going to be a cop like his uncle. When he was twelve his dad was stationed at Eglin Air Force Base, so they left New York and Buddy hadn't traveled much outside of Shalimar since.

Buddy finished reading an article about the decreased murder rate in the surrounding New York neighborhoods and took from the desk drawer an earmarked copy of *The Deep Blue Goodbye*. Sometimes, he worked on his own novel, a detective fiction piece that he was writing for the last eight years, but most times he read as a way to distract himself from thinking that in those eight years, he only wrote seventy-three pages. Before he could finish the first page of the McDonald book, he got a call from the chief.

"There's a reported robbery in town, off Old Ferry Road. Scott and some of his men are already over there gathering information. You'll be alone on this one."

It wasn't a homicide, but it would do. Buddy lifted his round body out of the chair and pulled hard on his shirt to stretch it over his belly to tuck in. He looked at himself in the mirror before he left the station to make sure his badge was shining and his mustache was neatly combed. He wondered for a brief moment if he should change and go as a plain clothes investigator, but he liked the way he looked in uniform.

Buddy drove up the long, winding gravel driveway to a large two-story home nestled in the center of large oak trees. He could see Choctawhatchee Bay behind the house. Two patrol cars were already there. Walking up to the front door, he straightened his belt, made sure his gun was in place, rolled his shoulders back, and took a look at the sky, ready to make the men in his family, the ones retired from keeping order in the world, proud. He knocked on the door. Another officer opened it for him.

"Hey there, Scott. I'll be taking it from here. Give me everything you've got and you're dismissed," Buddy said. Scott was one of the newest guys on the squad, having come from the Miami Tactical Narcotics Team, and didn't have the Shalimar gut yet.

"We know this is your case. We were just the first to respond to the call, so calm down, Piggy."

"Very well," Buddy said and walked into the living room where the family was sitting. The father, graying up top but still fairly young looking, stood to shake his hand. Buddy introduced himself as Detective Herring. The officers hid their smirks. The wife sat on the couch. Buddy thought he noticed a nipple showing through the white robe and quickly looked away. The daughter was sitting at the dining table answering questions from another officer.

"Can I get you a drink, officer?" Mr. Reynolds asked.

"It's detective, but yes. I'll take a Ginger Ale," Buddy said.

"I've got Sprite."

"Sprite's fine."

Buddy listened and took notes as Scott told him the situation. Mr. Reynolds sat a drink on the coffee table.

"You can save your pad," Scott said. "It's all here." He flashed Buddy his pad.

"Well, you know me, I like to double-check everything," he replied. The other cops laughed, even the one across the room who was interrogating the girl.

When Buddy heard how much money was stolen he

asked for the amount again.

"Jesus Christ, that's a lot of money," he said and took a sip from the Sprite. "What were you doing with twelve-thousand dollars in the house without a safe?"

Mr. Reynolds held his head low. "I know. I know. It was stupid."

"Why'd you have that much money?" Buddy repeated. "I mean…"

"Look, it's your job to find the money."

Buddy sobered up. "Carry on."

He and the other officers went into the bedroom from where the money was stolen. Scott looked around, making sure the parents were out of ear shot.

"That chick in there is one hot piece, isn't she Buddy?"

Buddy ignored the comment.

"I'm just saying, I'd fuck her so hard…"

"Hey, come on now." Buddy's face turned pinker. "That's someone's daughter you are talking about."

"It's always someone's daughter, dumbass."

"Well, if you can't stay focused, I'm gonna ask you to leave."

The other officers headed out, leaving Buddy to dust for prints on the doorknobs in the master bedroom.

"Mr. Reynolds, could you come in here for a second?" Buddy said.

"Yes sir?"

"Are there any firearms in the house?"

"Yes, downstairs."

* * * *

Charlie was sitting in his bedroom recounting the money that Vick left in his tip jar the night before. Two thousand dollars. He couldn't believe it. They found the money last week after Katelin's party, but he didn't think Vick would really take it.

After Katelin left for work, Charlie told Vick and Dustin how nice her parents' bedroom was and they went in, looked around, and became curious about the rest of the house. Downstairs was an office. Charlie flipped through some papers on the desk.

"They own some car washes or something?" he asked.

"Know what? She said something like that last night when I asked how they got so much money," Vick said.

They looked through the drawers. There was a handgun in the middle drawer. Vick picked it up and aimed it at Dustin's head. "Look at this thing. I've never seen a gun like this." It was a .357 with an ivory grip.

"Cut that shit out," Dustin said.

Underneath the gun, they found a Polaroid of a woman in red lingerie. "That's Katelin's mom?" Charlie said holding it up for the other two to see.

"Her mom's as hot as she is," Dustin said. "I bet he videotapes her." After a slight pause, Charlie placed the picture back where he found it, and Vick placed the gun on the picture. The three argued about the exact way it laid on top of the picture and then they raced upstairs to search every crevice of the parents' bedroom. Vick searched the bathroom, Dustin the dressers, and Charlie took the walk-in closet. Charlie felt a shoe box on the top shelf and looked inside.

There was no video, or any cheap Polaroids. Inside the shoe box, he found two overstuffed bank pouches. He threw the pouches on the bed and the other two boys stood watching as Charlie counted out seventy-two hundred dollars. They each took turns saying what they would do with the money. Charlie would quit his job at the airport and go somewhere tropical and surf until dawn every day. Dustin wanted to spend the money at a strip club and buy whores. Vick suggested they could buy some more cocaine, turn the seventy-two hundred dollars into twenty or thirty thousand dollars and then buy some whores to take with them to the tropics. They all agreed that was the best plan.

"Who's gonna take it?" Charlie said.

"I'm not," Dustin said.

"I will," Vick said. "Just a little bit. They won't even know any is missing." He stuck three hundred dollars in his pocket, and they rubbed their shirts on everything they touched.

A couple of days went by before Katelin invited Vick to come out to see her again. Her parents were due home later that night. They had sex, and while she was in the shower, Vick, with so much money tempting him, took a chance. He sprinted to the bedroom, grabbed the box, shoved the pouches around his waistline and while putting the box back, felt another box. Inside were two more pouches. He placed the four pouches in the trunk of his car, keeping one one-hundred-dollar bill in his pocket. He went back inside just as Katelin was stepping out of the shower.

He took her out to lunch that day at the most expensive

restaurant he knew: The Olive Garden. She told him he didn't have to.

"It's the least I can do," he replied.

A few hours later, Vick was back home in Pensacola. He went to Dustin's house and they counted out $12,100.

"Wanna go shopping?' Dustin said.

They drove to the mall and bought clothes, a Playstation, and a new stereo for Dustin's car. Then, they surprised Charlie at work with a two-thousand-dollar tip. He thought about giving it back to Vick that night, but told himself he would sleep on it. When he woke up, he couldn't remember why he put the money under his pillow.

* * * *

Katelin's father didn't sleep that night. He asked Katelin if she told the officer everything. She said she did. He woke her up early to talk about it some more.

"Who the hell are these guys? Why'd they come all the way from Pensacola?" he asked.

"They are just some guys I met," Katelin said.

"And they stayed the night?"

"They were too drunk to drive home."

"Take it easy, Steve. You're upset," Katelin's mom said. She knew that her daughter was already having sex, but she promised her daughter not to tell her dad. She openly talked to Katelin about birth-control and safe sex.

There was a knock on the door.

"Good morning, Mr. Reynolds," Buddy said as he walked into the house. "Morning Katelin. We've got a lot to discuss."

"Should I put on some coffee?" Mrs. Reynolds asked.

"That'd be fine."

"Donuts, too?" Katelin said under her breath. Buddy gave her a sideways glance.

"Last night I was thinking," Buddy licked his finger, thumbed through his notepad, and cleared his throat. "Now, if I'm not mistaken, you…" he pointed to Katelin.

She rolled her eyes at him.

He continued, "You said there was a party. And those three guys from Pensacola stayed the night."

"Yes. We've established that," she said.

"Now Katelin," Buddy said. "You're a suspect, too. Don't get too smart with me."

"What the hell are you talking about?" Mr. Reynolds shouted. "Don't bring my daughter into this. Go arrest them damn kids."

"Let me explain." He paused, careful about how he worded his thoughts. "Those boys are obvious suspects and I'll be talking to them, especially…" he thumbed through his notes again, "Charlie, the one who stayed in the bedroom. But we have to clear your daughter's name first."

* * * *

Tracy was a serious man. His cautiousness bordered paranoia. That was the only way he stayed ahead in his line of work. His clients never knew his true name. They only called him T. He rarely left his small, dark one-bedroom house. His windows were not only shielded by blinds and curtains, but he also hung blankets over them. It wasn't unusual for T to make people take off their clothes upon entering his house.

Cocaine was his business, and he was one of the top distributers in the Escambia-Santa Rosa County area. He only dealt with certain clientele. They had to be ambitious people. People like him who wanted to maintain a low profile and move merchandise quickly. They had to subscribe to his motto - No flash, just cash. Guests weren't permitted, and he wasn't pleased when rat-faced Jeremy showed up a few days ago with Vick. T stood firm, his arms crossed waiting to hear the explanation.

Jeremy hid his cowardly eyes behind his shaggy blond bangs and said, "I wanted to introduce you two. I've gotta move with my mom back to Sullivan and Vick wants in."

"Who the fuck you think you are? You quit, fine. But I can find my own do-boys." T spoke with a smooth and elegant voice. He never spoke louder than barely above a whisper, but his words lingered in his listener's ears well after he finished talking.

"I thought I was helping you out."

"What do you have to say?" T asked Vick.

Vick just looked at T.

"Nothing?" T asked.

Vick shook his head.

"Maybe I could use you."

T thought Vick knew how to keep his mouth shut. What he didn't realize was Vick didn't say anything because he was frightened of a six-foot six black man who towered over his rather fragile frame. T's forearms were as big as Vick's thighs, and the vein that pulsated from T's neck was as big as Vick's index finger.

"If you fuck up, it's both your asses."

A few days later, Vick knocked on T's door unannounced. Dustin and Charlie stayed in the car. Vick was snatched by the collar, ordered to lift his shirt, and take off his shoes. T frisked Vick starting with the socks and ending between his legs, making sure to squeeze extra hard around the balls. Vick grimaced but didn't squeal.

"I thought I told you not to just show up. I'd be in contact with you when I was ready to collect."

"No need." Vick handed T a bank bag.

"You rob a bank?"

"Close. I need more, lots more."

"You made this off that little bit I gave you?"

"Sure."

T pulled a gun from his waistband, pressed it up against Vick's right nostril, and said, "You fuck me over, I'll shoot the snot outta your nose." He held the gun there for a little extra effect. "Get them punks sitting in the car."

"C'mon, T wants to meet ya'll. He's gotta gun, though, so don't shit yourself if he pulls it out. Just be cool."

"What if he plans on using it?" Charlie said from the back seat.

Vick reached under the passenger seat, and stood up holding the ivory-gripped .357 in his right hand.

* * * *

"You want to clear my daughter's name?" Mr. Reynolds

said a bit too loudly. "Well, me too. And I'll help you." He stormed off into Katelin's room and began emptying drawers.

"Dad, you're acting crazy."

"Sir, this is not what I had in mind," Buddy said.

"This is so stupid. I didn't take anything," she cried.

Her dad then dragged the mattress onto the floor. A baggie of cocaine was on the box springs, probably less than a half-gram, but enough to raise suspicion with Detective Herring and piss off her parents. Katelin protested, but Buddy asked to speak with the parents outside separately. Katelin's dad looked as if Buddy hadn't been there he would've smacked her.

Katelin started cleaning up the room and was upset with herself for accepting the cocaine from Vick. She didn't even do drugs, but she thought it would make Vick like her more. Buddy walked back into the room and questioned her. He believed her when she said it wasn't hers. She was reluctant to say whose it was, but he convinced her it was necessary to clear her name.

Katelin could hear her parents arguing in the living room.

"How could she be doing drugs?" her mom said.

"And having guys sleep over," her dad added.

"She told you they slept on the couch. Well, except for that creep who slept in our bed."

"If we didn't find the drugs, maybe I could believe that."

* * * *

Dustin and Charlie sat on the couch in T's living room. A cross hung on the wall above the television set, and a picture of a muscular black Jesus hung on the cross behind them. T took Vick into the back room.

"Jesus is making me paranoid," Dustin said. He then pinched the head of his dick through his jeans.

"What's wrong with you?" Charlie asked.

"I gotta piss," Dustin said.

"Go then."

"Nuh-uh. T said not to lift an ass cheek off the couch."

"Pussy."

"You go then."

"I don't have to piss."

Forty-five minutes later, Vick came into the living room wearing a backpack. Dustin was hunched over, still holding his dick. T let them leave without a goodbye, good luck, or God bless.

Vick drove and Charlie called shotgun.

Dustin grabbed an empty YooHoo bottle that was rolling around on the floorboard and relieved himself in it.

"How much is in there?" Dustin asked from the back seat and tossed the piss-filled bottle into someone's yard.

"Can we try to be fucking professional. I don't know about you guys, but I don't feel like going to jail," Charlie said.

"Yeah, we need to be serious with this shit in the car," Vick said, sobering up. "Can we go to your place?" he said to Dustin.

"Hell no. My mom's home."

"What about your place?" Vick said to Charlie.

Charlie stared out the window.

"Charlie!" Vick shouted.

"What?"

"What about your place?"

"Whatever," Charlie said and turned his attention back out the window. He watched the passing of abandoned shopping centers, convenience stores on every corner claiming to have the largest beer selections and best prices on cigarettes. They passed the three hole-in-the-wall bars all within walking distance of his neighborhood. Tennis shoes hung across the power lines at the entrance to his trailer park like a welcome sign. Two stray dogs wandered, lost and hungry, and a couple shoeless diapered kids looked just as lost and hungry as the dogs. They passed trailer after trailer all with green scum climbing up the sides and knee-high weeds and finally passed the park, which was a broken-down swing set and a turned over slide.

* * * *

Charlie's mom worked the express checkout line of the supermarket. It was the same line she worked since moving to Pensacola when Charlie was seven, the same year her husband walked out on her. She left for Pensacola after he abandoned them and Charlie stayed behind with his grandmother in Sullivan. Leaving Charlie in Sullivan was the toughest decision she ever made, but they saw each other often, and Charlie grew to understand that moving to Pensacola was for work and to eventually create a better life for her and Charlie. It wasn't until after high school that Charlie moved down with his mother.

On her lunch break a co-worker sat down beside her.

"You okay, hon?" Marcy asked.

Charlie's mom pushed her hair away from her heavily bagged eyes. "I don't know," she said.

"Charlie giving you trouble again?"

"One minute it seems like he will be fine and the next, he's back to being the same ol' Charlie."

"What'd he do this time?"

"Didn't go to work today. He's getting too old for this shit." She paused long enough to shake her head. "When's he gonna learn to stick with a job?"

"He will, sweetie. Sometimes it just takes people longer to figure things out."

"I keep telling myself that." She took a sip of diet soda. "You know, when he was twelve, he told me, 'Momma, when I finish college, I'm gonna get a good job so you won't have to work this stupid one anymore.' That was six years ago. I bet he don't even remember telling me that."

* * * *

At Charlie's house, on a full length mirror that he took from his mom's bedroom, Vick laid out the quarter-pound of cocaine. T told them that it was still seventy-five percent pure. T received it at ninety percent and then cut it a little, but left some room for his distributers to play with some of the numbers so they could make as much money as they wanted. But it was never to drop below forty percent. They didn't know what he was talking about. They just remembered T saying to use some baking soda and laxatives. Dustin went to Eckerd Drugstore to get the ingredients while Vick and Charlie divided out some lines.

T gave Vick a new, never used, pre-paid pager to use only for communication with clients, and while Dustin was gone, he got his first page. By the time Dustin arrived, he had four appointments.

"We got a lotta work," Vick said. "Charlie, you keep chopping it up. Me and Dustin'll go for a drive."

"Why can't I cut?' Dustin asked.

"You're driving. Now write this shit down." He waited for Dustin to find a pen in Charlie's room. "So, we started with four ounces, right? After cutting, how much do we have?"

Charlie told him, "Six ounces."

"Holy shit. Did we over cut?"

"I don't fucking know."

"Okay," Vick repeated. "Shit, I can't do math. Hold on…" He took a deep breath. "Okay. We will sell eight balls for a hundred and seventy-five dollars. Grams for eighty. You writing this down?"

Dustin said he was. They all did another bump. "Okay," Vick continued. "And if someone wants an ounce, what? A thousand?"

Charlie nodded. "He gave us four ounces for twenty-five hundred. We should be okay."

"How much we gonna make on all this?" Dustin asked.

"Shut up," Vick said. "Let's get going."

The first order was to an apartment in the government housing projects. It was for an ounce, and it was probably going to be cut even more and resold as crack.

"Shit. Just one more of these and we break even," Vick

said. "We're gonna be rich, motherfucker." He cut out a line onto a cassette case, and they took a bump with Vick holding the cassette case and straw and Dustin leaning over to snort it while driving.

The second order was for an eight-ball to some high-school kids from the Catholic school. The next one was a one-gram deal to a doctor they recognized from a billboard.

* * * *

Buddy was in his office with the chief, a big man with an overpowering presence, but he and Buddy got along well. Probably because Buddy was one of the few who took protecting Shalimar serious.

"Buddy," the chief said. "Inconclusive results on the fingerprints around the bedroom. Everything clean. Don't think this was some kids. It seems they know what they are doing. Have you questioned them about repairmen or housekeepers or pool boys? Anything of that nature? We may be dealing with professionals."

"Well, so are they," Buddy said.

The chief left and Scott walked in.

"What's up, limp dick? What'd the boss say?"

Scott moved the pencil holder, stapler, and coffee mug around on Buddy's desk.

"Please don't do that," Buddy said.

"Do what?"

Buddy moved the items back in their proper place and continued, "The fingerprints didn't reveal…"

"Who gives a shit? Some punks rob a house and you act like you were just assigned to track Butch-fucking-Cassidy."

"To these good folks, it's just as important."

"Whatever," Scott said. On his way out he tilted Buddy's conduct award so that it hung slightly off-center.

Buddy walked over to straighten the plaque and then looked at himself in the mirror, wondering what approach Travis McGee would take on this case.

* * * *

When Scott worked down in Miami, he got involved working for a man named Renee Cortana. Scott became a police officer thinking it would be an easy way to be a corrupt scumbag and get away with it. Let chicks out of speeding tickets for sexual favors or maybe steal some drugs. Meeting Renee was fate.

It happened six years ago when Scott, only in his second year, made a routine traffic stop for what he said was an improper lane change. It was really because he saw a brown person driving a Corvette and thought for sure he was a drug dealer. In this case, he was right. Fourteen kilos in the back seat.

Although trained to approach vehicles differently, Scott's unchecked cockiness caused him to walk up to the window and knock. The window slowly lowered and the barrel of a shotgun slid out of the opening. A voice said, "Keep your hands on the car. My friend here is going to get out slowly, come around to you, and walk you to the other side of the car. Today isn't the day to be a hero."

Scott was escorted to the passenger side and paused briefly when he saw the cocaine in the back seat. He was then ordered to sit down in the passenger seat.

The skinny driver was Renee, and he placed the cold barrel of the shotgun into Scott's ribs and said, "I'm not looking for trouble. This is my job. And I know you've got a job to do, too. Sometimes two people doing different jobs can come together and make both jobs easier. I also believe in fate." He paused.

"Look hombre…" Scott started to say.

"Shut up," said the man standing outside the car. "We are not your hombres."

"No, you shut up, T. Let this man talk," Renee said.

"Yes, sir," T said.

"Continue," Renee said.

"I don't care what's in the car. Just give me a couple of bucks and we can both be on our way."

Renee sat quiet for a moment. "You think it is that easy, huh?"

"I'm hoping so."

"Give T your wallet."

T took Scott's wallet and pocketed his driver license.

"We know who you are, Officer Scott," T said. And then read the address to him. "And we know where you live."

"Does eleven hundred cover it?" Renee said.

"It's a little short for what you're hauling. How about I get some of that?" He motioned with his head toward the drugs.

Renee smiled. "Yes, yes. That is a good idea."

Scott then moved up north when Renee began to expand his enterprise. Renee wanted him in Pensacola, but at the time, Shalimar was the closest he could get. Renee eventually recruited top officials of the DEA, ATF, and policemen in sixteen counties. With help from people like Scott it was easy to stay one step ahead.

* * * *

Charlie's mom left work early because she wasn't feeling well. She didn't expect Charlie to be home, but when she opened the door, it was Charlie who was the more surprised.

"Mom! Why're you home so early?"

"Why didn't you go to work?" she responded.

"I wasn't feeling well," he said, sweat beading on his forehead and upper lip. "I was just getting ready to take a nap."

He couldn't get to the hallway without passing his mom and he knew she would stop him for a hug and to feel his head for a fever. He tried to sneak by while she was still taking off her shoes, but she caught him, one shoe still on.

"Wow, you're sweating," she said. "Go on to bed. I'll be there in a minute with some aspirin and check your temperature."

"I'm fine. I'm just gonna take a nap. I'll be all right."

He hurried to his room, locked the door and stared at the piles of cocaine. Orders number five and six were both eight balls. Number seven was another ounce. Things were easier than expected, except now they had to find another place. His mom knocked on the door.

"Ma, I said I was all right."

"I know. I was just wondering where my mirror went," she said from the other side of the door.

"What mirror?" Charlie said.

"The one from my room."

"Oh, that one." Charlie paused. He tried to shove it under his bed, but more than half of it was still visible. "It's in here. I borrowed it." Charlie was looking for the phone to call Vick.

"Can I have it back?" his mom asked.

"I'm in bed right now, ma. Can you get it later?"

He was still searching for the phone when he heard it ring on the other side of the door.

He heard his mom say, "Charlie is my son, and I have a right to know what this is about. Hold on a minute."

Charlie wondered what the hell Vick was telling her.

"Charles, get out of here right now. Why is the police calling you?"

* * * *

Vick and Dustin rode around in Dustin's blue '88 Ford Tempo that now had a stereo in it worth more than the car. Neither of them ever held that much of money. Vick never worked at a job for longer than three months. And Dustin never worked. Vick sold just enough drugs to support his habits, and his parents worked too much to notice or drank too much to care. Dustin was milking his grandparents for an allowance by going to a junior college, but his grandparents didn't know he was failing every class. He was never home long enough for them to ask.

Vick was in the passenger seat spreading out more lines on the cassette case as they drove back to Charlie's house.

"I'm gonna call T and tell him how we're doing," Vick said and they pulled over to a gas station to use the pay phone.

After the third try, T finally picked up and said, "Hang up the phone, you fucking idiot. Drive your ass over here if you want to talk."

"Hello. Hello. Damn, dude hung up on me," Vick said. "Let's call Charlie."

Vick looked over at Dustin still in the car. He was licking the cassette case. "Cut it out," Vick said, and walked over to him, smacking him on the side of the head.

* * * *

"Katelin, your mom and I've been talking…" her father said. Both her parents stood in the doorway.

"I know. I heard. You think I'm a whore."

"You watch your language. I never said that."

"That's what you're thinking, though. I heard you."

"What the hell am I supposed to think? You have three guys stay the night, then we find cocaine in your bedroom, and twelve thousand dollars missing from our room."

"Stay calm. She needs our support right now," Katelin's mom said.

"I don't have to stay calm, Sarah. We found fucking cocaine in her bedroom. How the hell do I know she isn't sleeping with guys to get it? I've read about cocaine addicts. They do that kind of stuff."

"Oh my God. I can't take it in this house anymore."

Her father's face reddened. He took a deep breath and turned around, leaving her mom to deal with her.

"I'll take a drug test if he wants, Mom. I don't do cocaine. I never have."

"I know, sweetie. He's just upset."

* * * *

Charlie went to get the phone, but locked his door from the inside so his mom wouldn't get the mirror. She wasn't thinking about the mirror anymore.

Charlie spoke into the phone: "Yeah, I was at a party in Shalimar. I don't remember her name. It could've been Katelin. Yeah, I slept in her parents' bedroom. Cause the couch was uncomfortable. I didn't take any money." He paused and then said, "What the hell did they have that much money in their house for anyway? A lie detector test?" Charlie looked at his mom and she was shaking her head no. He hung up the phone and told his mom Detective Buddy something, Herring maybe, was accusing him of stealing money and now wanted him to take a lie detector test.

"Tell him, he can kiss your ass. We need to talk to our lawyer."

"We have a lawyer?"

"No, but he doesn't know that."

Charlie smiled. Outside he waited for Vick and Dustin to return. His mom came out to ask why his door was locked. He told her it must've happened when he rushed out to get the phone. He'd get the mirror for her as soon as he went back inside. Charlie rubbed his tongue on the roof of his mouth. He wanted another bump. He sat on the porch steps and then stood up. He bit his nails, ran his fingers through his hair, bit his lower lip, sat back down, stood back up, chewed his tongue, sat back down, and finally decided to go inside for another bump.

Vick and Dustin pulled up into the driveway before he opened the door. He hesitated and then went to meet them at the car, stopping them before they got out.

"Why's your mom here?" Vick said. "And why was your phone busy?"

"Guess who I just talked to?"

* * * *

Later that night, T was entertaining some lady friends when he heard a car pull into the driveway. He opened the door before the kids knocked. He pulled Vick by his collar.

"What are you doing calling this number?" T said.

"I just thought…"

"You thought nothing. You don't know me. I don't know you."

Dustin and Charlie stared at their shoes while T berated Vick. "And what'd I tell you about bringing these knuckleheads over here with you?"

"They're my partners…"

T yanked a gun from his waistband and pressed the barrel to Vick's penis.

"Remember what I said'll happen if you fuck up?"

Dustin continued staring at his shoes. So did Charlie, but with a slight grin.

"On a lighter note, I heard you're doing good. People said your shit is way better than that bullshit they were getting from Lil Jeremy."

They followed T into the living room. Two topless women were snorting cocaine off the glass coffee table.

"What the hell are you listening to?" Dustin asked.

"Don't you know Charlie Parker?" T replied.

"No," Dustin said.

"That's unfortunate," T said. "But what's more unfortunate is what's going to happen to you if you keep looking at me like that."

"How am I looking at you?" Dustin said.

"Like you're retarded or something."

"That's just how he looks," Charlie said.

T smiled. "I like this kid."

Charlie nodded toward him.

"No need to be John Wayne, buddy." T winked at Charlie. "We're all cool here. Have a seat." T motioned to the couch.

Charlie sat on the couch. Dustin was transfixed on the women's breasts.

"You looking at my women?" T said to him.

Dustin jumped. "No, sir."

"Why not?"

T put his arm around Vick's neck to lead him toward the bedroom. His biceps tightened causing Vick to gag, but he tried to play it off as a cough.

"You know, you can do all right in this business if you keep your head on. Stop fucking around with those guys."

"Yes, sir," Vick said.

T laughed and loosened his grip and glanced back at Charlie and Dustin sitting quietly on the couch.

"What do you have in mind tonight?" T said as he shut the bedroom door behind them.

"I want a whole kilo for myself," Vick said. T sat on the

bed and put his head in his hands.

"Get out of here. You can't move that kind of weight."

"How much will it cost?" Vick said.

"You'll have to drive to pick it up."

"Okay. How much?"

"To Key West."

"Okay. How much?"

"Do you know where that is?"

"The tip of Florida."

"Yeah. Do you have any idea how long it will take you to drive there?"

"I don't know. Five, six hours?"

T laughed. "Yeah. More like fifteen."

"Whatever. How much?"

"You going to drive for fifteen hours with kilos of blow in your car?"

"I don't care."

"Do you know what kind of jail time that will get you?"

Vick shook his head no. "How much?"

"Fifteen grand."

"A half key?"

"Nine."

"Let's do that."

"If you make that drive, you getting some for me, too, you know?"

"I get paid for bringing your portion back, right?"

"You'll get paid."

"Let's do it."

"I'll take care of everything. You just have to drive," T

said.

As Vick came back from the bedroom, Charlie and Dustin had their noses in a pile of cocaine.

The next morning a knock woke Vick up. He looked through the eye-hole and saw a short, fat, pink headed cop. He let him in with the knowledge that it's better to lie to their face than to run like you have something to hide.

"You Vick?" the cop said.

"Sure am."

"Detective Buddy Herring," the officer said, extending his hand.

Vick turned around without shaking it and said, "Come on in." He offered the cop a seat at the dinner table. "Just about to make breakfast. You like bacon?"

"Hold off on the breakfast, smartass, and have a seat with me. We'll cut to the chase."

Vick sat directly across from him. Detective Buddy Herring drilled off questions about the night of the party, about his relationship with Katelin, and then asked where the money was.

"You're assuming I took it?"

"That's what Charlie said. You confess now, might save you some trouble."

"Okay, I'll tell you the truth," Vick said.

"Hold on a minute," Detective Buddy said. He took a tape recorder out of his pocket and pressed the record button. "Detective Buddy Herring speaking with Vick Strutton. Go ahead."

"Ready?" Vick asked. Buddy nodded. "I went to a party

to meet some girls. I met one. Fucked her. And that is as much as I know about her. You said her name was Katelin and that sounds about right. As for the money: I don't know nothing about that. Well, I do know if you are gonna have that much cash at your house, a safe would be a good investment."

"Anything else?" Buddy asked.

"No. Anything else you need, sir?" Vick asked and then stood up.

"Just one more thing…"

"Anything else, and you'll have to talk to my lawyer."

* * * *

It had been three days since the cocaine was found in Katelin's bedroom. Her dad made an appointment with a counselor. He wanted her tested and admitted to outpatient treatment.

"You gotta be kidding," she said.

"Not one bit."

"I'll take a drug test just to prove you wrong. If it comes up negative, I'm not going to counseling," she said.

"Yes you are."

"Or what?"

"Or you find somewhere else to live."

"Fine," she said.

"Fine," her father said.

Her dad went downstairs to his office. He sat back, opened the drawer to look at the picture of his beautiful wife, and noticed his gun was missing.

* * * *

Vick waited for a phone call from T with the details

about the run to Key West, but Katelin called first. She told him everything.

"So that's why the cops showed up here, huh?"

"I'm sorry. Really, I am. I told them that I know it wasn't you. I told them you were with me the whole time. That you couldn't have done it. But because your friend slept in my parents' room, they think it was him."

"That's fucked up. It could've been anyone at that party. Have they questioned anyone else?"

"I don't know," she said.

"Well, I guess we shouldn't talk to each other until this blows over then."

"Actually, I was hoping I could stay with you a little. My dad is flipping out and I can't stand being around him."

"No way. They'll definitely think we are in on this."

"I won't tell them I'm with you. They won't know."

Vick did like having sex with her.

"Okay," he said.

* * * *

Dustin picked up Charlie on the morning they were leaving for Key West. "What did you tell your mom?" Dustin asked.

"I told her I was going to Jacksonville to surf. She didn't think it was good idea with cops calling and all, but I told her I didn't have anything to do with it. That I was going so I wouldn't get harassed. She said, be careful. What about your grandparents?"

"I didn't tell them. Cops haven't called me yet. I figured it'd be best if I was gone when they do."

Dustin rolled a few joints for the trip, and he lit one in Charlie's bedroom while Charlie packed.

"Why the hell are you taking duct tape?" Dustin asked.

"You never know."

"Fucking boy scout."

"My passport, too."

"You're a weirdo."

When they arrived at Vick's house another car was parked in the yard. Katelin sat on the couch.

"Dude, what the fuck is this?" Dustin said.

"What?" Vick replied.

"She isn't coming," Charlie said.

"Yes she is," Vick said.

"Fuck that," Dustin said. Vick boxed him in the left ear. Charlie smirked. "Look," Vick said. "T arranged us a hotel, and she'll hang there while we get what we need. No big deal."

Dustin was bent over, holding the side of his head.

"T won't be cool with that," said Charlie.

"We ain't gonna tell him."

* * * *

Nearly a week passed since the robbery and still no leads. The chief told Buddy to give it a rest. If anything suspicious comes up, he could check it out then.

Buddy sat in his office pondering his options. He was sure those boys from Pensacola were involved. They seemed too cool about it, he thought. Scott then disrupted the brainstorm.

"Fat boy, I just heard about it. It's too bad. Guess you

just weren't meant to be a detective."

"The case isn't closed. Just giving those kids time to screw up on their own."

"Face it, it's a busted case. Give the kids some credit. They scored a good caper."

Scott left Buddy's office and again tilted the frames on his way out.

"That never gets old, does it?" Buddy shouted as Scott walked away. Scott lifted his hand and stuck out his middle finger. After a few more minutes of brainstorming and a cup of coffee, Buddy called the chief to ask for a week's leave.

"Buddy you've needed a vacation for a long time," the chief said.

* * * *

Katelin waited for the boys to return when her daydream about sunbathing by the hotel pool in Key West was interrupted by a loud knock. She looked out the eye hole and saw Detective Herring. She then hurried to the back door, locked it, and drew the shades in the back of the house. She huddled on the couch out of sight, wondering how he already knew that she was there.

Buddy walked around the house peeking through all the windows and even checked the back door. He became concerned when he drove by Vick's on his way to Dustin's and saw Katelin's car in the driveway. He filled up his gas tank before staking out the house a couple of blocks down the road, parking the car on a corner street. He could see the house with binoculars.

* * * *

Vick, Dustin, and Charlie returned to pick up Katelin. Vick handed Katelin the brochure that T gave him regarding the motel he reserved for them.

"The Back-Door Motel," she read. "1100 Washington Street, Key West, FL. We are located on the Atlantic side of Old Town, two blocks from the beach and three blocks from world famous Duval Street. Shopping, fine dining, and sightseeing are all within walking distance." She looked up and said, "Oh, I wanna go snorkeling while we're down there."

"Did you tell her why we are going down there?" Charlie said.

"No shit. She acts like we're going on vacation or something," Dustin added.

She glared at the two of them and over at Vick. He looked at Charlie and Dustin and shrugged his shoulders. Charlie smirked.

"Oh, and guess who came by while you guys were away on your secret boys-only mission?" When none of the guys spoke up, she told them.

"Fuck him," Vick replied.

"Now we really look suspicious. He's gonna think we all planned this together. Hope you know what you're doing, Vick. I guess we should get going before he comes back around," Charlie said.

* * * *

Buddy watched the kids leave the house and followed far enough behind that he wouldn't be noticed, but close enough to keep them in sight.

Things didn't change for a long time. A really long time.

Two and half hours later, still on I-10 when the car he tailed pulled over in Tallahassee, he was able to use a payphone to call the Reynolds' and let them know what was going on.

When the kids stopped for gas near Lake City, he filled his tank from the station across the street. He rushed into take a piss and made it out before they left. He called again as they stopped after merging onto Florida Turnpike S exit 328 near Orlando.

At that point, Buddy's bladder didn't cooperate with him anymore. He stopped and couldn't catch back up. Buddy called to say that he lost them and made the long drive back with the thoughts that maybe Scott was right: he didn't have what it took to be a great detective.

* * * *

Three hundred thirty-seven miles after exit 328, Vick pulled the car into the parking lot of the Back-Door Motel. Katelin slept with her dirty feet on the dashboard, Dustin with his head smooshed against the window, and Charlie wasn't sure if he slept at all. Each door of the motel was painted a different pastel color. Palm trees lined the parking lot. Their room was a two-bedroom suite with a kitchen. The walls were an off-white that matched the micro-suede sofa. The master bedroom had a hot-tub in the bathroom. The bed covers were tacky floral resort wear. Dustin and Charlie flipped for the second room. It was a twin bed with a painting of the Hemingway House hanging over it. Dustin lost and slept on the couch. After fifteen hours of driving and running out of cocaine around Miami, by the time they lay down, all four were asleep in seconds.

The next morning, they were awake by eight-thirty. The meeting was set for ten at a waterfront cottage with a guy named Renee. Charlie was still in the bathroom brushing his teeth while the others waited in the living room. Vick took the gun from his backpack and placed it into his waistband. Katelin saw him.

"You're taking a gun?" she asked.

Vick nodded. "This is the real deal, doll," he said.

"Whatever," she said. "Leave it here." She reached for the gun.

"What the hell is your problem?" Vick said, shoving her back.

"Let me see it," she said, reaching again, this time knocking it down his pant leg. He shoved her again, this time hard enough that she fell to the floor.

"You son of a bitch. Never lay your hands on me again," she said.

Dustin rolled on the couch laughing and shouted for Charlie to come in and watch. Vick readjusted the gun in his waistband and Katelin saw it clearly, the custom ivory grip.

"You robbed my dad."

"Busted," Dustin said.

"What the fuck makes you say something so stupid?" Vick said.

"The gun, you asshole. You don't think I know my dad's gun? I've shot that thing enough to know it when I see it."

Vick smiled at Dustin. "I'm sure it's just a coincidence, baby."

Dustin laughed again. Charlie came from the bathroom

and leaned on the doorframe of the living room, watching quietly, sipping from his watered down ice tea from the night before when they stopped at a Burger King.

"Bullshit, let me see it then."

"No time. We gotta go."

She lunged at him. Vick backed up.

"You son of a bitch," she said, throwing a few wild punches at him. She landed one on Vick's arm. The other two boys watched, but didn't stir.

"Bitch, you better back the fuck up," Vick said, backing up himself. Katelin grabbed the remote control off the table and hurled it at him. It struck his right eye. While he was hunched over holding his eye, she kicked him in the head. Vick stumbled back. She came at him again, but was quickly on her back after being struck in the forehead with the butt of the gun. She wasn't out cold, but wasn't in any position to fight back, either.

"Holy shit, man. What the fuck is wrong with you?" Dustin said. He wasn't laughing anymore.

"I don't have time to mess with stupid shit like that," Vick said.

"There was no reason for her to be here anyway," Charlie said.

"Fuck you, I'm running this," Vick said.

"No. Fuck you," Charlie replied. "What is your plan for her now?"

"Give me a second. I'll think of something."

Charlie went to the bedroom and came back with the duct tape.

* * * *

The boys stopped at the gate of a grand waterfront mansion.

"Some cottage," Charlie said.

"This the right place?" Dustin asked.

"T must've been sarcastic," Vick said. "This really is the real deal."

Two security guards approached the car.

"I'm Vick. Here to meet with Renee."

They waived the kids through the golden gates where a beautiful mocha-skinned lady was waiting for them at the ten-foot mahogany doors.

"Look at that Mexican slut," Dustin said as they walked up the driveway. He carried the backpack of cash.

"How do you know she's Mexican?" Charlie asked.

"Who gives a fuck where she's from? Look at them titties."

"Will you two shut up?"

"Don't tell me to shut up," Charlie said.

"My bad, dude," Vick said.

"And don't tell me to shut up anymore either," Dustin said.

"Shut up," Charlie said.

She led them down a marble hallway decorated with crystal chandeliers twelve feet above them. On opposite walls were two massive portraits of a scrawny man with his arms outstretched in a Christ-like fashion, one with a foreign flag behind him and the other with the American flag. Vick and Dustin followed directly behind the woman to the pool, which was shaded with palm trees and equipped with a floating tiki bar and five or six gorgeous ladies bathing in thong bikinis. Charlie lagged a little behind admiring the house.

The skinny man, the man from the portraits, but not nearly as handsome as in the pictures and not nearly as much hair, lounged on the patio. A gold chain hung down his caved in chest and a scar ran across his sweaty stomach. A woman massaged his feet, and another his upper thighs. Three men stood around him with automatic rifles. He called the boys over and shook their hands. They then stood back awaiting instructions.

"Welcome, gentlemen. I am Renee. T has said good things about you boys."

"Thank you," Vick said.

Charlie didn't say anything or smile. Dustin couldn't conceal his excitement and looked around with a stupid grin.

"What's wrong with him?" Renee asked.

Charlie nudged Dustin in the arm.

"What is wrong with you?" Renee asked again.

"Nothing," Dustin said. "It's just…nothing…I mean…look at this place. Look where we are."

Vick rolled his eyes. Charlie smirked. Renee began to laugh.

"It's like Scarface," Dustin said.

"Yeah. Just like Tony Montana. I like that movie. Even though it is pretty unrealistic."

"Best fucking movie ever made," Dustin said.

"Shut up," Vick said.

"This kid is crazy, no? I like him. He's like a little jester.

Tell us a joke, jester."

Dustin thought for a minute. "How are Michael Jackson and caviar alike?" Dustin said.

"He was just kidding," Charlie said to Dustin. "I think he wants us to stop talking."

"You must be Vick?" Renee asked.

"Not me," Charlie said.

"I'm Vick," Vick said.

"What is your name?" Renee asked Charlie.

"My name is Jackson," Charlie said and Vick and Dustin looked at him quickly.

"That is not your name, is it?" Renee asked.

Charlie shook his head.

Renee looked at Vick and then said, "He is the smart one, but you are the one in charge? So why did you bring this other guy. He is stupid and you are stupid for bringing him."

Vick was silent.

"It doesn't matter," Renee said. "It's too late now." He then ordered the girls that were massaging him to get the boys some drinks.

While Renee talked, Dustin leaned over and whispered to Charlie, "The way T talked about this guy, I was expecting some real gangster motherfucker, and instead, we get his little retarded brother."

Charlie shook his head and ignored him.

Renee leaned up on his elbows, and instructed them to sit, enjoy the daiquiris, the warmth of the Key West sun and the fabulous scenery of girls in string thongs.

"You can get used to this life, no?" he said.

Vick nodded.

"Hell yeah," Dustin said.

Charlie closed his eyes and ignored the question.

* * * *

Buddy was now passing Live Oak again. Tears rolled down his cheeks. He called Mr. Reynolds and told them that he lost the car. Mr. Reynolds suggested contacting other police officers in the area to be on the lookout, but Buddy explained there was nothing he could do. The kids hadn't committed any crimes.

"They goddamned robbed me. What the fuck do you mean they didn't commit any crimes?"

"I understand your frustration, sir," Buddy said.

Buddy continued down the highway talking to his deceased father:

"What do I do now? I screwed up. I was given an opportunity, and I blew it. Maybe I wasn't cut out to be a cop. I think it's time to hang it up. Maybe I was meant to be a writer. I could take six months off and finish my novel."

* * * *

Renee finished his drink, stood up and said, "Now we do business." He led them into the enormous Florida room. Large screen TVs, another bar with a bartender, enough indoor plants to run his own nursery, a pool table, a DJ spinning records to an empty dance floor, and a hot-tub off to the side. The three men with assault rifles brought up the rear as they walked in.

"You kids a bit young for this line of work. But I know T and he said you are his men. It just doesn't make sense.

Get naked."

Dustin began undressing. Charlie and Vick looked at each other. The three men with the guns stood behind the boys.

"Don't look so stunned," Renee laughed. "I said I know T. But I don't have a fucking clue who you three clowns are." The armed goons laughed with Renee.

"Uhh, sir," Vick said. "I've got a gun in my waistband, if you'd like to get it."

"Idiot," whispered Charlie.

"Wait, why're we getting naked?" Dustin asked standing in his boxers.

Renee laughed. "I don't give a shit about a gun. I know you wouldn't be stupid enough to use it. I'm looking for something else."

Vick swallowed. He looked at Dustin. Dustin shrugged. He tried to look at Charlie, but Charlie hadn't taken his eyes off Renee. Renee looked at Charlie and smiled.

As the boys began removing their clothes, Renee continued, "I was young in this business, too. A gun gives you confidence. And you need confidence if you want all this." He lifted his arms in a similar fashion to that in the portraits. "And this is what all of you want. I understand that. I remember when T was just a kid. He came down here just like you guys. Could've had this by now. But look at him. He's scared. A pussycat. Are you boys scared?"

The three of them stood completely naked. Vick said, "No, sir." Charlie slowly shook his head no. Dustin slowly shook his yes.

"Put your clothes on." While the boys dressed he continued, "Vick, you could do it. I see it in your eyes. You want it." He then looked at Dustin, "But you. You're too stupid." He then looked at Charlie, "And you…" Charlie stopped dressing and looked him in his eyes. "You just don't give a shit, do you?"

"Not about having this," Charlie said and looked around the house.

"I like you," he said to Charlie. "But not that much."

Charlie continued dressing.

"Here's the deal," Renee said. "There is no deal. I don't trust T anymore."

"What?" Vick said louder than he should have. "I've got fifty thousand dollars here and you're gonna tell me to just forget it."

"Yes," Charlie said. "That is exactly what he is saying. Just forget it. Let's go."

"Fuck that," Vick said. "T sent me down here to get something for him. What am I supposed to say when I show up and don't have his delivery?"

"Fuck T," Renee said. "He's got a little more to worry about than some petty shit like you."

"Petty shit? Like what?"

"Like if God forgives motherfuckers like him."

"What does that mean?"

There was a moment of silence. Charlie looked at Vick. Renee said something in Spanish and the DJ and bartender left the room.

"What's happening?" Dustin said.

"Vick, I'm going to teach you a valuable lesson," Renee said. "If you want to make it in this business, don't hang out with idiots like him." The guy standing behind Dustin switched the rifle to his left hand and pulled a smaller hand pistol from a hip holster. Vick and Charlie jumped as they heard the gunshot and saw the front of Dustin's head explode as the bullet entered. His limp body crumpled to the floor. His mangled head made a hollow thump as it hit the tile. The dark, almost black, blood quickly flowed from the wound.

* * * *

The doorbell rang. T turned down his stereo. "I thought you were finished and moving away," he said when he opened the door and saw Jeremy standing outside. There was another guy with Jeremy.

"I am," Jeremy said. "But before I go I needed to introduce you to somebody. This is Alex."

T looked at Jeremy. "You motherfucker." He then motioned for Jeremy and Alex to enter.

"How have things been, Scott?" T asked.

"No, man. His name is Alex." His voice cracked a little. "I...I just told you that," Jeremy said.

"Shut up," T said. "I'm so fucking stupid," T said to himself.

"What's going on here?" Jeremy said and swallowed.

"We all know exactly what is going on," Scott said. He lifted his right hand slowly from inside his jacket pocket and aimed a pistol at Jeremy.

"No," Jeremy said, and T could hear the realization and disappointment in Jeremy's voice.

Just as Jeremy began to cry, a quick white blast burst between his eyes.

* * * *

Vick and Charlie looked at Dustin's lifeless body. Renee laughed in the background.

"It's just business," Renee said. "You two are okay. You can relax."

Charlie took a deep breath. Vick stood motionless, tears welling up in his eyes, and then shouted "Motherfucker," as he reached for his pistol. Eight slugs pelted into his back.

Charlie took another deep breath and looked at his friends. Vick wasn't quite dead yet. His eyes flickered with the faintest sign of life. Charlie was pretty sure Vick was lying there about to die thinking he died a brave death. He often talked about that. But to Charlie, it was a stupid death. Dustin died a stupid death, and Vick followed.

"And you?" Renee said to Charlie.

Charlie dropped to his knees, interlocked his fingers behind his head, closed his eyes, and waited.

* * * *

Buddy arrived back in Shalimar and knew he should go see the Reynolds. He couldn't face them at the moment though. He went to the office and looked around, thinking he should start packing up. But couldn't face doing that at the moment, either. He was embarrassed. He wrote his letter of resignation and fell asleep. When he woke up, he burned his letter of resignation along with his novel.

* * * *

Charlie still waited. He opened one eye and then the

next. Renee stood over him.

"Get up," he demanded.

Charlie did as he was told.

"Forget about your friends." He motioned for one of his goons to take the book bag off of Dustin. "Give it to him," he demanded.

Charlie held it. Some of his friend's blood smeared onto his shirt.

"Take him to the airport." He then spoke to Charlie, "I suggest somewhere out of the country for a very long time. We will need to get him a passport."

"I have one," Charlie said. "I've been wanting to use it."

"Good. I never want to see you again. You never mention my name. If you do, I will know and I will find you after we go see your mother."

"You already knew who we were, didn't you? There was never going to be a deal, was there?"

"T was getting careless. I do not plan on hurting your mother. You understand?"

Charlie nodded.

"That is a lot of money for a kid your age. If you spend it correctly, you can do well for yourself. That is a good start on life. Most people never get that chance. Any ideas?"

"Costa Rica."

"Yes. Good. Now go."

Charlie turned and for the first time in his life he smiled uncontrollably. He was feeling true happiness, and at that moment of happiness, Renee put a bullet in the back of Charlie's head.

* * * *

A maid walked into room 216 of the Back-Door Motel. A loud thud came from the closet. The maid couldn't hear it over the sound of the music through her headphones and the vacuum cleaner running. The maid cleaned for maybe twenty minutes before she opened the closet to check the spare pillows and bed sheets and found a girl restrained with duct tape and dried blood streaked across her face.

Teacher of the Year

Hank stepped from his bed on the first day of summer vacation. His wife had already left for work at Emerald Coast Smile, where she was named Best of the Coast Dental Assistant. This was the summer, he said, where he was going to get his shit together. When he first started teaching, he wouldn't start counting down the days to summer vacation from the first day of school. He would at least wait until Spring Break. And even then, he sometimes felt guilty, although he knew all teachers secretly did it. If a teacher said otherwise, they were either lying or they were new teachers who were still idealistic enough to think they could change things. The ones who could penetrate the fascist walls of public education and could make every student they encountered creative, independent thinkers. Hank was like that his first few years, but every year he became less enthused, and by his fourth year, was teaching strictly according to union guidelines – 8:05am to 3:05pm with an uninterrupted thirty-minute lunch. For the past twelve years, after graduating college, he worked on a novel and made a promise to himself: this was the summer he would finish it, and he would begin querying agents. Teaching was never his goal. It was a back-up plan. The plan was to become a novelist.

He went out for the newspaper into the clammy south wind and thought what a great morning to ride his bike out to the beach and maybe get in a surf that was beginning to roll in from the low-pressure system down around the Yucatan. When his wife returned from work, they would pack up the car and begin the fifteen-hour drive to Jupiter where his wife's uncle owned a house and was allowing Hank and Rose to spend a month. It was to be his writing retreat, a gift from his wife because she knew how important it was for him to finish his book.

The thirteen-year-old who lived next door skateboarded in the driveway. He used to be called Timmy, but since he became a teenager he asked everyone to call him Tim.

"Morning, Tim," Hank said.

The kid mumbled and then said a little more clearly, "You going for a surf today, Mr. Hank? I heard it was supposed to be up."

"Was thinking about it. High school next year, huh?" Hank said. "Maybe you'll be in one of my classes."

"That'd be awesome," the kid said.

"Hope you like to read."

"Not really," the kid said.

"Hopefully, that'll change."

The boy's father walked out on the porch. He was a bit older than Hank, and they only really spoke on neighborly terms, never actually becoming friends. The kid's parents were church-goers, as they called it, and often times invited Hank and Rose to join them. Hank always said some other time. Hank had invited the boy's father over for barbecues, but after the first one the boy's father declined any further invitations because drinking whiskey and playing poker did not fall in line with Christian values.

"Say, you didn't get Teacher-of-the-Year this year, did you?"

"I didn't," Hank said.

"How many times they give you that, three or four times?"

"Just the once."

"Well, you'll probably get another one soon."

"No. I don't reckon I will," Hank said. He never realized how much work was involved after being awarded Teacher-of-the-Year, and there wasn't much in the way of return on the investment.

"That's all right. You got one. That's plenty more than most."

"I reckon that's so."

"Big plans for your summer break?"

"You could say that. We're driving down to Jupiter in a couple days for a month visit."

"That is a heck of a drive."

"It is."

"You renting a car?"

"We're taking the van." Hank owned a 1976 VW Westfalia camper.

"That thing going to make it all the way there?"

"Sure as hell hope so."

"Godspeed on your travels. Come on, Timmy. I need you inside."

The kid raised a hand in a feeble wave to Hank. Hank returned the gesture with a nod.

Hank set the paper on the counter top and walked out to the garage to get his bike. He had built a contraption that wheeled his surf board behind him for the thirteen-mile ride to the beach.

After the hour and a half bike ride over two bridges, the swell was barely knee high. He opted for a body surf session instead.

He drank coffee and ate a breakfast of scrambled eggs, grits, and wheat toast at the hot dog shop on the island.

Once home, he grabbed the newspaper and lounged out back in his hammock underneath the shade of two Magnolia trees. He read about a local boy who had recently been found dead of a heroin overdose while sitting in his car out at Ft. Pickens, needle still in his arm. The local boy was in the Navy and was serving lunch aboard a destroyer in the Yemen Sea when terrorists drove a boat loaded with explosions into the side of the ship. The local boy survived the explosion but couldn't survive the aftermath.

He had a habit of looking at the arrests and obituaries every morning. Looking for people he grew up with or students he taught. It never surprised him to see someone's name he recognized in there. Once he saw the name of a student of his, only fourteen years old, who was killed and then burned inside of a car. Another student of his was once arrested for shooting a man at a gas station that told him to pull his pants up. He thought back to when he was a teenager and a good friend, Charlie Gutterman, was killed down in Key West in a drug deal gone wrong. They found his skull and that of two others in the Everglades. About three years ago another of his childhood friends, Shaun Stallworth, was in the paper for robbing a bingo parlor up in Sullivan. He cut ties with most of the people he grew up with as their paths drifted apart, and he sometimes held on to a tinge of guilt for not staying in contact. He decided to see if Shaun still had the same phone number.

"What's up?" he said to the voice on the other end of the phone.

"Who's this?"

"Who do you think it is?"

"How the fuck do I know?" It was definitely still Shaun's number.

"It's Hank, asshole."

"Holy shit. Mr. Teacher-of-the-fucking-year? No, I don't want to buy any goddamn raffle tickets or sponsor any bullshit afterschool club."

"Funny," Hank said. "I'm on summer break and thought I'd catch up with you. It's been a while. Still at the same house?"

"The one you just called? Yeah, I'm here."

"You mind some company?"

"Sure. Come by. I've actually been thinking about you. Funny how the universe works like that."

"Is that so?"

"Come over. I'll catch you up."

Hank made the forty-minute drive north to Sullivan. After high school, Hank moved to Pensacola and attended the university where he met Rose and never thought once about returning to Sullivan. He drove past Mr. Rafferty's property and saw that the logging boxcar he lived in as a child was no longer there. After his father died, the trailer was unrentable and Mr. Rafferty had it removed.

He continued on to the neighborhood where some of his friends grew up, a neighborhood built in the early fifties when the paper mill opened. Now that the population continued to dwindle, the cookie-cutter neighborhoods were in disrepair as most of the homes were used as rental properties, except for the few old-timers who still hung around, refusing to die. If he continued on instead of turning into the neighborhood he would get to the correctional facility that employed about half of the population. The other half still lived below the poverty level. He thought of stopping by to see how Teddy was holding up, but it had been so long since they spoke, he wouldn't know what to say to him. Hank wasn't even sure if Teddy still lived in town or not. Last he heard, Teddy was divorced and moved back to Sullivan to start his own heating and air company.

Two tan Chevy Impalas were parked in Shaun's driveway. One had a black garbage bag duct-taped where the back windshield should be and the other had two flat tires. Shaun never moved out of his parents' house and his ailing father, who lived in a nursing home, had signed over the house to Shaun. Hank was overcome with nostalgia as he parked in the street and looked around at the unkempt yard, dirt where a lawn once grew and untrimmed bushes in what once was a flower bed.

This was where Hank first saw a boob when Shaun's older sister flashed him during a game of truth or dare. Last he heard of her, she danced at the Backseat Lounge in Pensacola. Shaun's house was also the first place Hank drank beer, smoked pot, snorted cocaine, tripped on LSD, ate mushrooms, and gotten laid. What was her name, Hank wondered? It was one of Shaun's girlfriends. He was fourteen, she was maybe fifteen, and Shaun asked her if she could change the fact that Hank was still a virgin. And she did while Shaun sat in the room on a beanbag chair playing Contra on the Nintendo. Hank still remembered the thirty-man cheat code to that game. Up, up, down, down, left, right, left, right, B, A, select, start. Hank smiled at the memory.

He shook his head and stepped from the car, happy that he was one of the lucky few who escaped Sullivan, even if by escape, it meant only moving an hour south to Pensacola.

Hank remembered another time that Shaun had been kicked out of the house. He stayed with Hank and they sat up talking about how they would never be like their parents. As kids, they couldn't understand how by the time people turned forty, they couldn't afford to live well. They didn't understand why their parents were poor. Now, as adults, it was pretty easy to see how that was possible. Shaun told him how he and his folks lived for two weeks in a car. Hank told him as long as they knew each other Shaun would never have to worry about where to sleep. Although, he was never sure he would always have a place to sleep.

Hank knocked and a couple seconds later an eye peeked through the blinds before Shaun opened the door.

"Damn man, can you knock any louder?" Shaun didn't wear a shirt to cover his basketball sized belly. He had tattoo of the Sullivan water tower the length of his torso, from his armpit to his hip. He stuck a hand down his jogging pants and scratched himself. He hadn't shaved in a few weeks.

Didn't look as if he combed his hair in about as long either.

"Good to see you, too," Hank said.

"You coming in or what?"

He followed Shaun into a dimly lit, smoky living room. It smelled like perfume made with cat piss and lavender. Twenty minutes and then I'm out, Hank thought. Beer bottles lined the coffee table, one still sweating. Clothes were piled on the recliner chair, and Shaun picked a wrinkled shirt and smelled it before putting it on. He tossed the rest of the clothes on the floor so Hank could sit down. A bearded man that Hank didn't recognize sat on the couch smoking a cigarette. Hank nodded hello. The bearded man continued to stare, unmoved. A football video game was paused on the television. The bearded man lit another cigarette from the butt of his last one. No one spoke and Shaun packed a bowl of cannabis into a glass bong before offering it to Hank.

"Thanks," Hank said.

Hank picked up the bong and took a toke. He coughed on the exhale. Shaun laughed. The bearded man didn't.

"Some good shit, huh?"

Hank still coughed as he nodded his head and then passed it to the bearded man.

"Can I get a drink?" Hank said.

Shaun motioned his head toward the kitchen. Dishes were piled in the sink. Hank looked in a couple cupboards and then Shaun said, "Grab one outta the sink and rinse it off. Or grab ya a beer from the fridge."

Hank looked at a couple of glasses in the sink, picking one that looked the least dirty, and smelled it. It smelled of eggs and he set it back in the sink.

"I'll get a beer," he said.

He opened the fridge and scrunched up his face at the mildewy smell. He cleaned the top of the beer can with his T-shirt before opening it.

"Come back here for a minute, Hank," Shaun said. "I want to show you something."

Hank followed him down the hallway.

"Why don't you clean this place up a bit?" Hank said.

Shaun stopped for a second, looked at him, and kept walking. "I'm moving out in a couple weeks. Place is getting hot, you know?"

"No," Hank said. "I don't know."

Shaun laughed. "I never thought you'd become such a square."

Shaun opened the door to the master bedroom. Bundles of marijuana covered the mattress.

"Haven't you been arrested for this before?" Hank said.

"Once. But that's how you learn. Right, Teach?"

"Not quite."

"It's cool. It'll all be gone in a week or so. That guy in there knows some people. He's taking two pounds off my hands today."

"That's a good chunk of change. But I just came by to say hey. I'll let you get back to work."

"Fuck that. I ain't seen you in a while, man. Let me give this dude his stuff and get him outta here, and me and you'll hang for a bit. Shoot some shit."

"I really should be getting back."

"That's fucked up, man. Just give me a sec. It won't be long."

Shaun gave Hank a small sack of pot. "On the house."

"I'm good," Hank said and tried giving it back.

"Just take it, man. I've got plenty. You're on break, remember?"

Hank put the bag in his pocket and left Shaun in the room. The bearded man passed him in the hallway. Hank sat on the couch and looked at his watch. A couple minutes later he did it again. He heard Shaun and the bearded man arguing in the room. He heard the bearded man say he didn't trust Hank. He heard Shaun tell the guy to get the fuck out of his house.

The bearded man scurried past the living room with a backpack. Shaun came back into the living room. "Making money, my friend."

"That guy was a bit sketchy," Hank said.

"Fuck him." Shaun picked up the controller and started playing the video game.

"So, what've you been up to?" Hank said.

"Same shit, man. Same shit. I've been doing this for a while now. When I'm finished I'll have about eighty grand saved. All cash. And I'm moving out of this town."

"About time."

"Got me a little one on the way."

"A little what?" Hank said.

Shaun paused the game and looked at Hank.

"A kid?" Hank asked.

"Yeah, man. A kid. A little girl. You believe that shit?"

"No. I don't believe it."

Shaun smiled, resumed the game, and started playing again.

"You keeping it?"

"Don't be an asshole."

"My bad. Congrats."

"Yep. My girl has family in St. Louis and we are going to take that money and start new. She's going to go to school and shit, and I'll take care of the kid until she gets a good job. She's going to be an x-ray tech or whatever they are called."

"You shitting me?"

Shaun shook his head. "Nah, man. I think I'm finally getting out of this. This time for real, you know. I've always looked up to you, man. You are the only one we grew up with that isn't a fuck-up. You were the only one that was ever really a friend to me, too. Like today. Just calling me up out of nowhere. I appreciate it, man."

"That's what friends do, right?"

"Friend, my ass. We're practically brothers."

Less than five minutes later three loud knocks thumped out from the front door. Shaun threw the controller on the floor and sat motionless. Hank held his breath and tried not to move.

After about thirty seconds that felt like much longer, Hank whispered, "Who is it?"

Shaun shushed him.

Then someone bashed open the front door and footsteps scurried down the hallway. Shaun bolted for the backroom and Hank heard someone yell, "Get on the floor."

Hank ran for the back door and was cut off through the other side of the kitchen by a SWAT team member with a pistol aiming at Hank's face.

"On the ground, on the ground, on the ground," the man yelled. Hank did as he was told. The man cuffed him and patted him down, pulling the baggie from Hank's pocket.

Rose picked him up from jail as he was released on a misdemeanor charge of possession, but he wasn't allowed to leave the city until his court date. She didn't even look at him on the ride home. He didn't want to look at her either. He spent the next two days in the house in a mix of borderline depression and embarrassment. When Rose went back to work, her coworkers already knew, having read it in the paper. He had yet to contact his principal. He didn't know if he would be fired or sent to a rehab program and was afraid to find out.

He didn't have to wait too long because his principal called him after a couple of days and said it would be best if he resigned. The school already received phone calls from concerned parents and he could try to fight it with a lawyer, but the principal thought it would be best if Hank stepped down on his own and maybe reapplied in a couple of years after it blew over. He would still get his summer pay.

"What do we do when the summer pay runs out?" Rose asked him.

"I'm going to look for work," he said.

"We can barely afford our bills as it is," she reminded him, squinting her eyes at him in disgust and shaking her head.

"I'll work two jobs if I have to."

"Who the hell will hire you?"

He found a job roofing houses.

When the court date arrived, he was given one year of probation for possession and he was required to complete an outpatient treatment program. His lawyer told him that Shaun was given eight years.

"For selling pot?"

"He told them you were in no way involved."

"I wasn't."

As their savings started to dwindle, Hank got a second job working at the burger joint down the street.

"Holy Shit. It's Mr. Ackerman," he heard one kid say in the backseat of a '96 Ford Explorer as it pulled up to the drive-through window.

"Man, you were the coolest teacher," the shaggy-haired driver said as he handed Hank the money.

The kids in the back giggled.

"It's fucked up you were fired just for some weed," the driver said. "How have you been?"

"I'm doing fine," Hank said. He brushed away a fly that buzzed about him for the past twenty minutes and stared out over the car through the Formosan termites swirling in the yellow light of the parking lot.

"What time you get off?" a boy in the passenger seat asked.

"In a little while." Hank glanced down and vaguely remembered the driver at school and wasn't sure if he ever taught him. A co-worker, not much older than the kids in the car, handed Hank the greasy paper bag of food and he held it out to the kids.

"You wanna get high?" The kids laughed.

"I'm all right," Hank said and handed the bag of food to them. As they drove off, a joint flew through the window and hit him in the chest.

On the way home, the news on the radio announced that the tropical depression in the lower Gulf would most likely form into a hurricane by the end of the week. The surf would be up in the next couple of days, but the construction crew he now worked for decided to work through the weekend to finish up before the storm. Surfing rarely crossed his mind anymore.

He turned the dial to the oldies station, pulled the joint from his shirt pocket, and pushed in the cigarette lighter. He thought back to the beginning of the summer and shook his head at the series of events. He smoked half the joint and put the rest out in the ashtray. At the house, his wife was already asleep. He made a peanut butter and jelly sandwich and opened a beer. It was nearly midnight and his ride to the construction site would be honking outside within five and half hours. He went to his writing desk, turned on the desktop, and pulled up his novel. He had thirty minutes to try and get some words on the screen before he needed to be in bed. If he knew this was how his life would've turned out, he would've been more serious about writing when he had the time. Now that he didn't have time for anything, it was all he could think about it. But instead of writing, he dozed off.

His wife joked the next morning that she would divorce him, but she couldn't afford a lawyer. Hank had the feeling she wasn't joking.

Roulette

Hank Ackerman was only thirteen years old as he watched life leak out of the head of Herman Ramos, a kid he barely knew.

Herman was rumored to make kids eat dog food if they refused to do anything he suggested. Hank had only been to Herman's house three times before. This was the fourth time. The first time he saw Herman's mom put a needle between her toes. Herman's father was in jail for stabbing a guy. That's what Herman told everyone.

Hank met Herman through Shaun Stallworth who told Hank that they could get nudie magazines and pot from Herman. Both Hank and Shaun had recently started smoking pot.

After taking a few tokes each out of a crushed-up RC Cola can, Herman brought out a .38 Special from under his mattress. Hank and Herman sat back on the bed and Shaun lounged on the floor.

Without saying a word, Herman put the gun to his head and pulled the trigger. The gun clicked. He laughed. Shaun chuckled. Hank was horrified.

"The cylinder is empty," Herman said.

"I know," Hank said. "I don't think you would be stupid enough to do it for real."

"You daring me?"

"Let me see it," Shaun said.

Herman held the gun and continued looking at Hank until Hank looked away.

"Come on. Let me hold it," Shaun said.

Herman handed it to Shaun and said to Hank, "You dare me to do it with a bullet in the cylinder?"

"No." Hank said. He wouldn't look at Herman.

"Don't dare me. Because I'll do it."

Shaun pointed the gun at Hank.

"Cut it out," Hank said. "It's not funny."

"He's scared," Herman said. He and Shaun laughed.

"I ain't scared, but don't be pointing no gun at me."

Shaun pulled the trigger. Hank jumped at the click.

Herman laughed. Hank looked up at him and had never seen a meaner looking kid.

"Did you see him jump?" Herman said. "He's a pussy."

"I ain't, either," Hank said.

"Then prove it," Herman said. "Let me see that gun."

Shaun handed it back to him and Herman reached in his bedside dresser, pulled out a handful of bullets, and set them on the night stand. He picked up one, inserted it, and spun the cylinder. He turned the gun around and held it out for Hank.

"Fuck that," Hank said. "This is stupid."

"You do it," Herman said to Shaun. Shaun took the gun, held it in his hands and seemed to contemplate it.

"What're you doing?" Hank said.

"He ain't a pussy like you. Are you Shaun?"

"You ever done it?" Shaun asked him.

"Yeah. I've done it. More times than I can count. I ain't afraid to die."

"Bullshit," Hank said.

"Give it here," Herman said. "I'll show ya. I ain't afraid of nothing."

Shaun handed it over.

"You going to do it for real?" Shaun asked.

"Don't do that shit," Hank said. "I'm going to go."

"Before you go, watch this," Herman said. He placed the gun under his jaw and smiled.

Hank shoved the gun down. "Stop fucking around," Hank said. "Put the gun away."

"Holy shit, man," Shaun said. "You are fucking crazy. You were really going to do it, weren't you?"

Herman smiled and said, "You have no idea." He then placed the gun in his mouth. He pulled it out and said, "Ever tasted the barrel of a gun when you know it's loaded?"

"I'm getting outta here," Hank said and turned towards the door.

He stopped with a hand on the door handle when he heard Herman say, "I should shoot you in the back of the head. Told you your friend was a faggot. Here watch this."

A loud crack filled the air. Hank was looking at a poster of a shirtless Jim Morrison with his arms stretched out like Jesus on the cross and didn't see the actual moment of death, but for the rest of his life Hank often times heard that gunshot in his dreams.

Summer Songlines

Rodney Helms, wearing only his swimming trunks, returned from the bar across the street from the beach with a frothy drink made from Crème de Cacao, ice cream, and rum. The drink in that part of Florida was known as a Bushwacker and he sipped his drink as he walked along the black asphalt of the Casino Beach parking lot, stepping on the white lines of the parking spaces when the soles of his feet could no longer take the heat. He sat underneath the canopy that he set up every morning for the past fifteen years to sell sunglasses. He kicked his feet up and stared out at the Gulf, watching as a few longboarders surfed the thigh-high waves next to the pier.

"Are you closed already?" a female voice said.

Rodney, not looking up, said, "Sun is setting soon. Not much use for sunglasses after that." He stirred his milkshake-like drink and took a sip, eyes still out at the Gulf.

"It's supposed to rise again tomorrow, though, isn't it?"

"What's that?" He looked up.

"The sun. It'll rise again tomorrow, right?"

"Hell, how am I supposed to know an answer to a question like that?" Rodney said.

The woman was in her mid- to late-thirties and stood with her chest pushed out displaying still perky breasts under a long, form-fitting, blue flowered sundress. Rodney touched a two-inch scar on his neck as he looked at her.

"I'll take these." She put on a pair of glasses and looked at herself in the little mirror that hung from the canopy.

"Take em."

"How much?"

Rodney couldn't take his eyes from hers.

"Have a drink with me," he said.

She looked at her watch, then at Rodney, and then back at her watch one more time.

"I can't right now. Meeting a friend for dinner."

"After dinner then?"

"How about I just pay for the glasses?"

"At least tell me your name."

"Lena."

"In town for a bit?"

She nodded yes.

"Then stop by and say hey tomorrow."

"Maybe." She turned and walked away. With her back turned, she lifted a hand to wave and shouted back to Rodney, "Thanks for the glasses."

Rodney watched her walk away and mumbled, "Thank you."

He then boxed up the sunglasses and broke down the pop-up tent. He carried it all to the back of his pickup truck, grabbed his surfboard, and walked down to the water to join those other fools who thought that surfing the Gulf of Mexico was still better than not surfing at all.

Afterward, he grilled a steak and set it on a plate that he carried inside and put on a TV tray. From the fridge he pulled out a bowl with a sticky-note attached to it that said: *Thanks for a wonderful night. Love, Isabella.*

Rodney crumbled the note and tossed it in the garbage

can. He scooped a large pile of coleslaw next to the steak and put the bowl back in the fridge before grabbing a beer and sitting on the couch in front of the TV tray. Behind him, hung a painting by his grandmother of a sailboat moored out in the water. She painted that shortly after her husband, his grandfather, died. It was maybe ten years old now. His grandmother died shortly after painting it. A lamp made from bamboo was on the end table next to his reading chair. His grandmother had made the lamp, too. Most of the things in the house were still as if his grandmother lived there. When his grandmother died, he quit his job in Miami and moved back to Pensacola to live in the house. She left him a pretty hefty inheritance. Money he never really knew she had.

His German Shepherd lay on an oriental rug in front of the TV. From his living room, Rodney looked out the sliding glass door at the swaying palm trees, took a bite of coleslaw, and with a full mouth said, "Goddamn, that girl can make some coleslaw."

He opened his beer and tossed the bottle cap behind him toward the direction of the garbage can in the kitchen and he held the beer up to make a toast, "Here's to it and to it again. If you ever get close to it and don't do it, may you be tied to it and forced to do it until you never want to do it again. So fuck it. Here's to it." It was a toast that he and his baseball buddies in Miami made up when he was in college. He took a long pull from the bottle and turned on the TV. A documentary about rumrunners and pirates. He knew about them all too well. He turned it to the Weather Channel.

"Storm is still coming for us, Cheeseburger. Just another

couple days," he said to the dog.

He cut into the steak and Cheeseburger lifted her head. He cut a strip of the fat and tossed it to her. Cheeseburger caught it and seemed to have swallowed it whole. Then she circled a few times on the carpet before finding a resting spot in the same place she was before.

"I'm going out for a bit, girl. Don't wait up."

Cheeseburger barked.

Jimmy's Beach Bar was the oldest bar on the island, dating back to 1952 when the first houses were constructed out there. For many years, the island was owned by the federal government, but in 1947, Fort Pickens was closed and a battle between conservationists and developers ensued. Gulf Island National Seashore was established to appease the conservationists and the developers started building small cinder block homes. But the developers couldn't get people to move out to the island and the first homes built were given away in the Fiesta of Five Flags' annual treasure hunts. Rodney's grandmother won one of the homes. James Mallory built Jimmy's Beach Bar, and Jimmy Mallory Jr. took it over in 1976 after his father died. Growing up, Jimmy heard stories that Mallory Square in Key West was named after someone in his family, but he never really looked into it. Very few cinder block homes survived from that era; most were replaced with large multi-family stilt homes sitting up on fifteen foot pilings, and the beach front was taken over by high-rise condominiums.

Bras and underwear hanging from the ceiling welcomed visitors to Jimmy's Beach Bar. It was easily the busiest bar on the island any day of the week. The pool table, the two shuffleboard tables, and the foosball table out back were already occupied with college kids. The band was into their second set, and a group of girls danced.

Rodney walked in barefoot wearing semi-wrinkled khaki shorts and an un-tucked Hawaiian shirt. His hair was slicked back, hanging over his ears. He squeezed next to Earl at the bar. Jimmy nodded and when he got a chance placed a beer in front of Rodney. Earl had four empty shot glasses sitting in front him. Earl was a big guy, just under three-fifteen.

"Hot Rod, you made it," Earl said.

Rodney tapped his beer bottle against Earl's.

"Earl, did you let those guys sitting around the dance floor know that the women will be fucking the band tonight?"

"Who you trying to kid, Rod Bone? We know you'll be taking a few of them home, too."

"I'll let you have them tonight, Earl. I'm on the lookout for only one. Her name is Lena. Any Lenas come in here?"

"Not that I've heard," said Earl. "Hey, Jimmy," Earl shouted. "Anyone by the name of Lena come in here?"

Jimmy shook his head no.

"She was a looker, Earl. But seemed familiar to me. I might know her from somewhere."

Rodney took a drink from the bottle, and when he was down to about half, Jimmy walked over and set another beer in front of him.

"What about me?" Earl said. "Another whiskey."

Jimmy poured a whiskey into a rocks glass and topped it with water.

"Hey now," Earl said. "You trying to tell me something?"

Rodney laughed. Jimmy ignored him.

"I never met a Lena," Rodney said.

"That you remember," Earl said.

"I remember most of them, buddy. And I definitely would have remembered her."

Jimmy said, "How about earlier, Earl? That lady came in and sat down next to you? The one that had you picking your jaw off the ground? What was her name?"

"I don't know. Excuse me fellas, but I do believe I have found my dancing shoes."

Earl stumbled out to the dance floor.

"Said she was in town looking for someone. Is that someone you, Rodney?"

"Ain't no one looking for me, Jimmy."

Rodney finished the first beer, took the fresh one sitting on the bar, and then slapped Earl on the ass as he walked past. Earl, sweat circles forming under his armpits, danced close behind one of the young girls. A few of the young guys standing around the dance floor joined in on the dancing as well, not wanting to let Earl be the only one getting close to the girls. Rodney set quarters down at the foosball table. One young guy at the foosball table with biceps larger than Rodney's thighs wore a crimson color university t-shirt and matching baseball cap. Rodney watched this kid play and every time the young college boy scored a goal he would turn to the girl next to him for a high-five. She reluctantly agreed to the high-five.

"What do you want old man?" College Boy said.

"Just a friendly game, buddy," Rodney said.

"You need a partner. Can't you see we are playing partners?"

"I don't need no partner, partner."

"We're playing for money."

"Good. I need some."

"Five dollars a game."

Rodney put his quarters in and laid a five on the rail. He scored as soon the ball dropped on the table.

"One – Nothing."

College Boy turned to the girl and grabbed her under the arm, "Grab me a beer, will ya babe?"

"You should be a little nicer to the ladies," Rodney said.

"Worry about playing the game, will ya?"

College Boy dropped the second ball in play and Rodney scored again.

"Two – Nothing."

The girl came back with a beer and sat at a nearby stool. She didn't watch the game. She watched the dance floor and swayed on the stool.

After four games, Rodney walked back to the bar counting his money.

"How'd you do?" Jimmy asked.

"Twenty bucks," Rodney told him.

The DJ announced a wet t-shirt contest. The contestants crowded the stage. Rodney watched College Boy's girlfriend walk onto the stage. Earl followed her on the stage.

"How much did he drink tonight, Jimmy?"

"He's been here since two. We should be in for a good

one."

The first girl was introduced and she stepped into the plastic kiddie pool. The DJ poured a pitcher of ice water over her. She gyrated in a pink thong and a ripped wife-beater undershirt.

"That's why I never wanted a daughter," Jimmy said.

"And that asshole over there," Rodney pointed to College Boy, "is why I never wanted a son."

Rodney then noticed Lena sitting in the corner. She looked at Rodney, smiled, and raised her eyebrows in a flirty way. Rodney held up his index finger to her, indicating for her to stay there. Rodney grabbed Jimmy by the arm.

"Look. That's her. Gimme an extra beer to take over to her."

"No can do, old bud."

Jimmy directed Rodney's attention toward the stage where Earl swayed back and forth, the crowd getting louder with each sway until Earl puked, splashing vomit on the feet and legs of the girl from the foosball game. She screamed and College Boy rushed the stage with clenched fists. Rodney looked back at Lena. She summoned him over. Rodney looked back at Earl, who was now being pummeled by College Boy. Jimmy ran around the bar, grabbing Rodney by the collar and pulling him towards the scuffle. Rodney and Jimmy squeezed through the crowd just in time to see Earl get knocked out by a stool. Rodney landed a punch on the back of College Boy's head, knocking him to the ground. Jimmy rounded up enough locals to sort out the rest of the brawlers. It took four men to carry a snoring Earl off the stage.

"Good hit," Jimmy said to Rodney.

"He was drunker'n hell. Anyone could've knocked him out."

They laid Earl out on a cot in the storage room behind the bar. Rodney helped clean up as Jimmy announced drink specials to quiet the restless crowd.

"Two-for-one shots of Cuervo for the next fifteen minutes," Jimmy said through a megaphone from behind the bar.

Rodney stumbled out of bed with the same shorts on as the night before and Cheeseburger jumped down to follow him into the kitchen where a young lady stood at the stove frying eggs. Her blond hair was pulled back and she wore a white t-shirt with no pants, showing off tanned, athletic legs.

"Scrambled fine?" she asked.

Rodney chuckled and said, "Morning, Isabella. Yeah, scrambled's good."

She smiled at Rodney, her youth not yet ruined by the effects of the sun or drinking at the island bars known for heavy pours. Cheeseburger waited by the sliding door.

"Let me take her out for a quick walk," Rodney said.

He walked Cheeseburger down to the beach. Rodney shielded his eyes from the morning glare bouncing off the water and studied the surf. Cheeseburger ran along the shore chasing birds and ghost crabs. Rodney whistled and Cheeseburger stopped and returned to Rodney.

"I'm going up to grab my board. Sit still until I get back."

Rodney jogged up the path between the sand dunes to his house. Cheeseburger followed behind him.

Isabella sat at the counter eating breakfast and said, "Some lady came by looking for you. Said her name was Lena. A hot one, Rodney." Then under her breath, "A bit old though."

"I heard that. Did you tell her I was down at the beach?"

"I told her, but she said she'd just find you later. Who is she?"

"Don't know. Met her yesterday. She didn't think me and you are together, did she?"

"Don't worry. Our secret is safe. I said I was the housekeeper."

"She believed you?"

Isabella shrugged her shoulders.

Rodney returned from his room with a surfboard.

"What about breakfast?"

"Later."

Rodney was the only one out at what he liked to call "his break." Sitting on his board, he splashed water on his face and rubbed some on the back of his neck. He caught a wave, riding it with a laid-back style reminiscent of the old days when surfing was still a counterculture, before it became fashionable and before people started to manipulate the waves instead of letting the wave do the work. He cross-stepped to the front of the board to hang five toes over the edge and placed his hands behind his back as he glided along the wave. A few dolphins broke through the surface out toward the horizon while a fever of about twenty stingrays swam below him.

Rodney stepped from the shower and Isabella and

Cheeseburger were stretched out on his bed. Isabella still wore his t-shirt.

"I'm off today," Isabella said. "Do you wanna hang out?"

"You can hang out with me at the sunglass shop."

"What do you even do that for? Not like you need the money."

"I like talking to people. Gives me something to do."

"Can't we hang out today?"

"People rely on me for their eye protection. I can't let them down."

"You're stupid. Are your glasses even polarized?"

"No." Rodney pulled on his shorts. "But they do offer one hundred percent UV protection."

"Sure you don't want to hang out?" She flashed him a breast.

"Don't you have some people your own age to hang out with?"

"You're hoping to run into Lena, aren't you?"

"I am."

"And if you don't you're going to come wake me up in the middle of the night again?"

"Is that what happened last night?"

"You're such an asshole."

Rodney sat on the bed next to her. They both pet Cheeseburger.

"I've told you, I'm twenty years older than you. We would never work."

"Twenty-three."

"What?"

"You are twenty-three years older than I am."

"Whatever. We would never work. I give you free rent and we keep each other company until you meet the man of your dreams."

"What if you're it?"

Rodney laughed. "You should be going to school. Meet you a handsome doctor or something. I'm nothing but a drunk. Just got lucky and had a fairly rich grandmother who left me a house on a sandbar."

"I told you I'm going back to school in the fall. And what do I need a doctor for. You're rich enough."

"Far from rich, babydoll. Just don't need a lot of income. Big difference."

"I don't need to be rich," she said. "And you're handsome enough. For now."

Rodney laughed.

"Different songlines, babe. They may have crossed, but don't merge."

"You and those damn songlines. I'm not sure you even know what that word means."

"Nah, but it sounds cool, right?"

"I'm going to visit my sister anyway. I'll come back when the storm passes. Go see how normal folks live for a while."

"Might learn something from her."

"Like what? How to work like a dog all day to come home to crying babies and an asshole husband?"

"All right. Just the work part, then. Might learn how to

work."

"You're one to talk."

She leaned in and kissed Rodney on the neck and then on the lips. Rodney reached up under the t-shirt and grabbed her breast, but she pulled back.

"I'll be back when the storm passes," she said.

Rodney entered Jimmy's Bar. It was empty except for Jimmy mopping the floor. Jimmy greeted him with a head nod. Rodney took a barstool from off the bar and sat down. He picked up the remote control and turned on the TV. He switched it to the Weather Channel.

When Jimmy finished mopping he walked up behind the bar and shook Rodney's hand.

"Nother scorcher, huh?" Rodney said.

"Okay with me. I've got AC and frozen drinks'll be selling today. You see that depression is now a tropical storm?"

"Hurricane then?"

"Maybe by tomorrow or the next day. But it's heading this way. We are directly in the center of the cone of probability."

Rodney and Jimmy sat for a while in silence watching the tropical update.

"Say, that twenty-two-year-old still staying out at your place?" Jimmy asked.

Rodney smiled. "Yeah."

"What do those young girls see in you?"

"You making breakfast or what?"

"I'm getting to it. Mango-Banana?"

"As long as you add some rum, I don't give a shit what

you put in it."

Jimmy pulled out fresh fruit from the cooler underneath the bar and prepared a smoothie in the blender.

"Guess who came by the house today while I was surfing."

"Lena?"

"Now, how would you know that?"

"Jimmy the Bartender knows everything that goes on around this hedonistic sandbar."

Rodney laughed. Jimmy set the smoothie on the bar. Rodney leaned forward and took a sip, not lifting it off the bar so as not to spill any.

"She came by this morning. I wasn't even here yet. Earl let her in. Said she was really something, too."

"She is. So, Earl told her where I live?"

"I reckon so, if I had to guess."

"Surprised he was awake after the shit-show he started last night."

"I heard that," Earl said walking up behind Rodney.

"I love you."

"Yeah, yeah."

Earl patted him on the shoulder and then kept walking to the bathrooms. Rodney took a couple more gulps of his drink.

"Well, let's see if I can make any money today."

"Don't work too hard."

"I'll do my best."

Rodney was reading a well-used copy of *The Mosquito Coast*. A woman looked at a pair of maroon, horn-rimmed glasses, the ugliest of the bunch. She wore a pastel pink one-piece and a light blue wrap cover-up around her rather large bottom half. Her face had the cracked mud look of way too much sun. Rodney looked up as she wiped away the sweat from between her sagging breasts. She then tried on the glasses.

"You should get those. They look fabulous on you," Rodney said.

"You think so?"

"Especially with that gorgeous outfit."

"I don't know."

Lena walked by flashing Rodney a coy grin and waved.

"Come on, lady. You want them or no?"

She put them down and tried on another pair.

"Just take any pair you like."

"Excuse me."

"Just leave eight dollars in this jar. Honor system." Rodney reached down and set a jar among the glasses.

"Really?"

"Yeah. I've got to go."

"Don't rush me."

The woman started searching through her purse. Rodney tried to follow Lena with his eyes as she began to fade into the crowd.

"You know what? They're free. Just take them."

"Are you sure?"

"Of course."

"Well, thank you, kind, sir."

"De nada."

A little blond-haired boy walked up and tried on sunglasses and Rodney grabbed him by the arm, not taking his eyes from the back of Lena's head.

"Make sure no one takes anything. I'll buy you an ice cream cone when I get back."

The boy smiled a gap-toothed smile. Rodney took his cash box with him and ran after Lena.

Lena stood in the sand, her sundress flowing in the breeze. She watched four young sailors play volleyball. The sailors were always easy to spot because of their haircuts. Rodney reached out to touch her shoulder, but before he did she said, "Business looks good today, Rodney."

He pulled his hand back.

She turned around.

"Hi."

"Hey," Rodney said back.

"Is Rodney Helms at a loss for words?"

"Do we know each other?"

"I stopped by your hut the other day."

"It's a shop. But what about before that?"

"I'm not sure you can call a pop-up tent a shop," she said with a laugh and directed Rodney's attention to a commotion taking place at the sunglass stand.

"Shit. Will you wait a minute?"

"No." She laughed again.

"You think that's funny?"

"Very much so."

"Tonight at the bar then?"

"Maybe."

"Nine-thirty."

"We'll see."

Rodney sprinted back to his sunglasses, shouting to the people, "That shit ain't free, you know."

Rodney pushed his way through the crowd. The little blond boy, sitting in Rodney's chair, played with a paddle ball, the kind with a little red ball attached to the paddle by an elastic string.

"Anyone who took sunglasses better give me some money unless they want to talk to the police about this."

A few people laughed as the crowd dispersed. The little boy still paddled away.

"Hey, kid."

The kid looked up. "I want vanilla with chocolate syrup, but no nuts."

"I ain't getting you shit, kid. Get outta here."

The little boy sulked away. Rodney sorted out the glasses and assessed his losses.

"Eighteen pairs. Goddamn savages."

A shadow moved across the table. Rodney looked up to see a bear-sized man with different colored beads weaved through his gray beard. He held the little blond boy in his arms.

"You make my boy cry?"

"Did you ask him why?"

"Yeah. Said you promised to buy him ice cream and now won't."

"Bullshit."

"Watch your language around my boy, or I'll make you

swallow your teeth."

"Words bad, violence good. Don't listen to your old man, kid. Violence is never the answer."

The man hit Rodney with a straight jab to the forehead that knocked Rodney to the ground. Rodney took a few seconds to collect himself and then used the table to hold him steady as he stood.

"Tell him what kind you want," the man said to the kid.

"Vanilla with chocolate syrup, but no nuts."

Rodney reached into his cash box and gave the boy two dollars.

"What do you say, Junior?"

"Thank you."

The man set his boy down, and they walked off hand in hand.

Rodney stepped out of his bathroom with a towel around his waist, and Isabella and Cheeseburger hadn't changed sleeping positions since the morning.

"Thought you were going to your sister's?"

Isabella looked up with a crease on her cheek from where she buried her face in the pillow while she slept and said, "I am. Didn't want to leave Cheeseburger alone all day. Left you some food in the fridge."

Rodney dropped his towel and pulled on his jeans.

"Thanks, babe. I've got plans though."

"With Lena?"

"Yeah."

Isabella jumped from the bed and inspected Rodney's forehead. She poked at the small goose-egg and Rodney pulled back.

"What happened?"

"Bumped my head."

"Did you put ice on it?"

"It's fine."

"Let me see."

"It's fine," Rodney said and moved to the closet, taking a collared shirt from a hangar. He smelled it before putting it on.

"Wow. Jeans and a collared shirt. Someone's smitten."

Isabella folded down his collar and kissed him on the cheek.

"I'll see you after the storm then."

Rodney started combing his hair straight back and looked at Isabella through the mirror.

"Be safe, sexy."

She smiled.

"Be good, Cheeseburger," she said and left the room.

Rodney walked into Jimmy's with Cheeseburger following by his side. The same band from the night before was setting up equipment on stage. The crowd was thin, mostly regulars that Rodney nodded to as he made his way next to Earl at the bar.

"Rod Mon," Earl said.

Jimmy set a beer in front of Rodney.

"Not tonight, buddy. A bottle of your finest wine."

"Nice touch," Jimmy said.

"Lena?" Earl said.

"You bet. I'll be in the corner. Can you bring the wine

over when you see her sit?"

"A woman your own age, huh? You feeling all right?" Earl asked.

With a smile, Rodney extended his middle finger to Earl, and took a seat at the table. Cheeseburger curled up at his feet underneath the table.

The crowd filled in. The band started their first set. Rodney sat alone.

"Brought you a drink, buddy," Jimmy said.

Rodney took a drink.

"What time you got?" Rodney asked.

"Ten twenty."

Rodney nodded.

"Want some food? Maybe some conch fritters?"

"Wine not?"

"So the wine too?"

"Wine more than anything."

Jimmy returned with two baskets of conch fritters. He set one down on the table and one on the floor. Cheeseburger immediately started in on them and Jimmy refilled Rodney's glass of wine.

"It's a hurricane now," Jimmy said.

"Yeah?"

"Should hit tomorrow evening, around two in the morning."

"I could use a good storm. Maybe it'll wash this whole damn sandbar away." Rodney looked at Jimmy. "Except for this place, of course. Ain't nothing can wash this son-ova-bitch away anyway."

Rodney put a conch fritter in his mouth. He bit into it and then held his mouth open, allowing the steam to escape.

The bar was packed again with college kids, most of the old-timers having left before the young folks showed up. The band went into their second set and Rodney finished the bottle of wine. Jimmy came over and sat next to him.

"You all right, buddy?"

"Of course. Not the first time I've been stood up. Won't be the last."

"Another bottle?"

"No. Going to get to bed and catch the early morning swell."

"Take care, friend."

Jimmy patted Rodney on the shoulder.

Rodney's alarm buzzed. Cheeseburger walked around the bed in a circle before lying in the same spot she slept in the entire night. Rodney swung his legs from his bed and pulled on the shorts from the floor next to his bed and entered the living room. He turned on the TV. Weather Man said, "Hurricane Francine, now a category two, is expecting landfall between Gulf Shores and Pensacola around one in the morning. Beach residents are being encouraged to evacuate."

Rodney turned off the TV. He opened the sliding glass door to calm winds. He went back to his bedroom and emerged holding his nine-foot surfboard.

Rodney was alone again, the sun having just come up. The first wave he rode carried him some thirty yards. He pulled out over the top as he approached the close-out section and paddled back out. On the next wave, he grabbed the rail, pulled into the pocket, and stayed crouched, dragging a hand to keep pace as the wave barreled over him. When he was spit out of the narrow opening he let out a hoot for no one to hear but himself and the Gulf.

Rodney paddled back out. Up on shore two guys studied the waves. One pointed to where Rodney surfed and they entered the water and started paddling out.

"Sixty goddamn miles of beach and you have to come surf right next to me," Rodney said aloud.

Rodney caught another wave and rode it into shore.

Inside the minimart, Rodney waited in the checkout line behind a dozen other customers. They bought the rest of the bottled water, enough canned food to last through several hurricanes, and batteries. Rodney held a case of beer in one hand, two bottles of wine under his armpit, and balanced a six pack of eggs on top of ribeye steaks in his other hand.

"Hey, someone who doesn't think it's the end of the world," the clerk said.

Rodney laughed. The clerk, a shaggy-haired boy not much older than seventeen said, "Catch the surf?"

"I did. You?"

"Hell no. I had to be here for the rush."

"Maybe if you're lucky you can get some of the leftover swell when it passes."

"I hope. Take it easy, Rodney."

The sun started racing toward the horizon. Rodney lounged in his hammock holding a beer in one hand and the Paul Theroux book in the other. Cheeseburger lay underneath him.

His neighbor, a retiree from Ohio just finished lowering storm shutters and Rodney decided he should probably lower his as well. He rolled out of the hammock and his neighbor walked over.

"Need any help?"

"Thanks, bud. If you want to grab those Sea Purslanes and take them in for me, it'd be great."

The neighbor took in the potted plants and then walked back out and said, "Think it'll be a bad storm?"

"Never can tell."

"Are you staying on the island?"

"Yep."

"You think it's a good idea? We got a hotel on the main land. You oughta consider leaving the island, Rodney."

"I'm sure I'll be fine."

"What'll you do if it gets bad?"

"Cook up steak and eggs before the power goes out and drink a bottle of wine. Watch the storm come in."

"Good luck."

Inside Rodney turned on the TV and put in a VHS copy of Bogart and Bacall's *Key Largo*. A tradition started with his grandparents. Within ten minutes, he was snoring on the couch.

Cheeseburger barked and woke him up. He opened the door to look out at the first bands of the storm coming ashore.

"Just the wind, girl," Rodney said to Cheeseburger.

Before sitting back down, he heard a knock too strong to be the wind. He opened the door just enough to peek out, and Lena stood under the porch light, her hair wet and strung across her face. Her dress soaked through and clinging to her breasts and thighs. Rodney stared for a moment.

"You going to make me stand in the rain?"

"I'm thinking about it."

"I can't come in?"

"My girlfriend might get mad."

"She said she was your maid."

Lena pushed the door open and entered. A puddle formed around her feet.

"A towel, maybe?" she asked.

Rodney continued staring.

"Look. I'm sorry about the other night," she said.

"I don't know what you're talking about."

He left her standing in the doorway and came back with a towel. He threw it at her and walked into the kitchen.

"Shower's down the hall, if you'd like."

Rodney put the steaks on the stove while she showered. Lena walked in wearing one of his t-shirts. Her hair was still wet.

"Found your maid's shirt in one of your drawers."

"Looks good. Beer?"

"Sure."

"Fridge."

Lena got out two. She opened them by placing the caps on the counter edge and popping her fist down on top. She handed one to Rodney. He took a long pull. Lena sat on a stool at the counter. Cheeseburger settled down by her feet.

"You want salad, too?"

"If it's no trouble."

"Get it out of the fridge."

She bent down to get the vegetables out of the lower drawer. She caught Rodney looking at her bottom sticking out from underneath the t-shirt. He didn't look away. She cut up the vegetables on the cutting board on the counter. He got out two plates and put a steak on each and slid a fried egg over top of them. She scooped some salad next to the steaks. They walked over to the couch. Rodney turned the TV to the Weather Channel.

Weather Man said, "Hurricane Francine's winds have reached category two strength. Tropical force winds have been reported from Mobile to Destin. Expect the weather to deteriorate until landfall, which is expected around ten p.m."

The lights flickered. The television flashed off and then came back on. The wind howled louder. The shudders trembled. Then the lights went out for good. Rodney lit some candles.

He looked at Lena, who was even more beautiful in the glowing light. He rubbed the scar on his neck.

"Wine?" Rodney asked.

Lena nodded yes. Rodney went to the kitchen.

"About last night…," Lena started.

"That was last night," Rodney said.

Rodney brought back the bottle and filled two glasses nearly to the rim.

"Look, I was scared. I just couldn't tell you," she said.

"Come on."

"I was a bit embarrassed."

Rodney waited. She looked away.

"Shy all of a sudden?" he said.

"I was embarrassed that you didn't remember me."

"I'll take that to mean I should."

"I guess not."

She moved closer to Rodney. She tucked her hair behind her ears and sipped her wine. Rodney topped it off.

"I was only seventeen," she said.

Rodney chuckled and took a big sip from his glass before topping it off.

"Just a few years ago then," he said and winked.

"You were twenty-two, I think."

"I haven't been twenty-two in a long time."

"You were a fisherman. Just graduated from the University of Miami where you played ball on scholarship. You were trying to decide whether to move back here or continue living in Miami."

"I was a deck-hand, yeah, for most of one season. But baseball was a long time ago. I went back to Miami for a few years and became a schoolteacher. Tried my damnedest to play ball. Just wasn't in my cards, I guess. How do you know all this?"

"That's how you got that scar."

"No, some silly girl… No shit?"

Lena laughed.

"Are you messing with me?"

Lena shook her head no and then said, "I didn't think you would forget me after I hooked your neck."

"It took me a long time to."

They both drank the wine.

"When I left you said you would never forget me. Back then, I believed those kinds of lies."

"Back then, I believed things I said."

A loud thunder cracked outside. Cheeseburger ran to the bedroom.

"You said you'd write. Said you'd come visit. I almost dropped out of college that first semester to come back to you. But you ignored every attempt I made at contact."

Rodney shrugged. And topped off the glasses again.

"I knew it was just a matter of time before you met some college-going kid and wouldn't want anything to do with me," he said.

"I did meet one. But I still thought of you."

"I never told a girl I loved her until you. You broke me down good. And then left a month later."

"College was important to me. What did you expect?"

"That's why I didn't say anything."

"Please. You said all kinds of things. You said, who needs college? You said we could move to Costa Rica. You said you had a rich grandma that would die soon and leave you a house on the beach."

Rodney lifted his hands and looked around. "That part I wasn't lying about."

"You had this crazy scheme worked out about moving over there and running some kind of surf camp."

"I was serious about that."

"I know, but I couldn't do that. That wasn't me."

"Well, that's why I ignored your calls. We were two

different people."

"Don't give me that 'we were on different songlines' bullshit either."

Rodney laughed. "It's true though. You wanted the city life."

"What if I said not anymore."

She leaned in to kiss him. Rodney kissed her back. She pressed in harder, forcing Rodney on his back and then straddled him. He reached under her t-shirt and pulled it off of her. The storm intensified.

Rodney woke up to the sound of Lena's voice, not directed at him. He kept his eyes closed and listened in: "Hey honey, I'll be flying in today," she whispered into the phone by the bed.

A short pause.

Lena continued, "I know, but all flights were grounded yesterday because of the storm."

Another pause.

"Still at the hotel."

Pause.

"Look, I'm already running late. I'll be home shortly."

Pause.

"Okay. Love you, too."

She hung up the phone. Rodney clapped.

"Nicely done," he said.

"Will you let me explain?"

"Some breakfast before you leave? Maybe some coffee?"

"Fuck you, Rodney. I've wanted to divorce him for a

long time. I just haven't been able to tell him yet."

"Why bother? Poor sap probably already knows."

"Can I speak? Or have you already made up your mind about me?"

"You can speak. Do I have to listen though?"

Rodney went to the kitchen. She followed behind him. He smelled a glass in the sink and then drew some tap water into it and drank it down, looking at her as he drank.

"You're not a child anymore. You don't have to act like you aren't hurt. I had business here, but I came looking for you."

"How sweet."

"Can you not be an asshole for two seconds?"

"That's asking a lot."

"I don't know why I thought you would be any different. The last few years I've really been thinking a lot about you and how I screwed up. I wanted to see if I found you, if we still had that old spark. Last night was perfect. I've played it safe my whole life. I was ready to finally take a risk. Maybe go to Costa Rica."

"You took a hell of a risk."

Rodney walked out the front door to assess the damage. A few fallen palm trees, but nothing too tragic. The wind already shifted out of the north.

"If I stick around. Get an apartment out here. You think we could try it out again?"

"Are you serious right now?"

"Yes. I didn't want you to hear that. I thought I could fly home and I would tell him I wanted a divorce and then move here. Things didn't quite work like I planned."

"They never do. I'm going for a surf. I'd suggest you get on a plane and go back to your husband. It'd probably be best if he doesn't know about last night."

Lena sat on the couch, watching Rodney as he took his surfboard from the room and headed out the back door.

"Just like that?" she asked.

Rodney stopped and looked at her. "Unfortunately, yeah."

Rodney came in from surfing and Lena was gone. He set the surfboard on the floor and picked up the phone.

"Isabella. Hey babe. Storm wasn't bad. You coming back today?"

Pause.

"What do you mean she can get you a job?"

Pause.

"What about our plan to open a surf camp in Costa Rica?"

Pause.

"Of course I was serious."

Pause.

"I thought you hated living in the city."

Pause.

"Costa Rica would be a change of scenery, too."

Pause.

"When later? Why can't we talk now?"

Pause.

"Fine. We'll talk later."

Rodney hung up the phone and looked at Cheeseburger.

"Goddamn it, you better not plan on leaving too. Let's go back to the beach?"

Rodney and Cheeseburger walked back to the beach. Cheeseburger took off ahead of him to chase crabs and birds and Rodney walked along the water's edge, picking up seashells every few feet to toss them as far out to sea as possible.

Alright Guy

"Hey, want to make some money today?" That was the first thing Rodney Helms said when Hank Ackerman answered the phone.

"Heard you were unemployed," he then said.

"You heard right." Nearly four months ago Hank lost his job as a high-school history teacher. He roofed houses for a couple weeks, but construction was down across the region and he hadn't roofed a house in two weeks. The next job lined up was a week away. He flipped burgers on weekend nights, but couldn't get any extra shifts.

"Got a job for you if you want. Easy money."

"What is it?"

"Had to cut away an anchor in the storm last night. Need someone to get down in some scuba gear and find it. I've got the coordinates of where I left it. After we get the anchor, I've got some people coming to hangout on the boat. Need someone to play bartender. I'll pay you seventy-five dollars for five hours of work."

"I'll do it."

Hank's wife, Rose, was at work and it was only nine-thirty in the morning, putting him home well in time to scoop out the litter box, wash the dishes, and have dinner ready. At the moment, keeping the house clean was pretty much his only responsibility.

Rodney sat at the outdoor bar and although he was older, he looked in much better shape than Hank.

"What is this?" Hank said. "Five or six already?" He

was referring to the Bloody Mary Rodney was putting to his lips. He sat next to Rodney.

The fellow sitting on the other side of Rodney said, "Damn, he knows you, huh?" His name was Eric – tall, lanky, red hair. Eric started in high school by screen printing t-shirts in his parents' garage and later started shaping surfboards. Now, he owned the premier surf shop in town.

Rodney's dog, Cheeseburger, recently passed away, and he sold his grandmother's house on the island so lived on his sailboat, a forty-foot Pearson named *Sure Thang*.

"How do you guys know each other?" Eric asked.

"We've known each other a long time," Rodney said.

"Rodney got me my first job when I moved down here from Sullivan," Hank said.

"That's right. I was going back to Miami and trained you to be a deckhand to take my spot. Shit. Nearly forgot about that."

"Rodney was good friends with my older brother, too."

"How is Teddy? Haven't heard from him in a while. He ever tell you that Puerto Rico story?" Rodney asked Hank.

"I've heard it," Hank said.

"Poor guy just never seemed to catch a break. How is he?"

"I think he's back in Sullivan. We don't talk much anymore."

Rodney leaned in and whispered to Hank, "It's really only my third." He held up his Bloody Mary and winked. "I'm not that big of a lush. But I did smoke a joint the size of my thumb. Get you a beer?"

"You paying? You said I can drink all I want."

"You're not on the clock yet." Rodney winked at him.

"When do I get on the clock?"

"When the girls get here."

"What about the anchor then?"

"As soon as I finish this we'll go. I know exactly where it is. It won't take long. What're you drinking?"

"Don't worry about it. I'm walking across the street for cigarettes."

Hank looked out at the water and saw Rodney's boat. It was anchored about fifty yards off shore. He never docked his boat at the bars because that cost money. Instead, he anchored it off and rowed his dinghy to shore.

Hank had twelve dollars in his pocket. He bought cigarettes and a High Life tall boy. Part of him regretted going out there, but another part of him said he was earning money to help with bills. But really it was mostly an excuse to get drunk. The kind of drinking he was about to embark on was good for the soul, he told himself. It flushed his system. Allowed him to start over. Charles Bukowski said getting drunk was like a form of suicide where you're allowed to be reborn again. Hank thought that was a bit sensational, but he agreed it did do something to him. Something he felt was necessary on occasion. Something he rarely found elsewhere. He found it while surfing when he was younger. Before surfing he felt it at church once or twice. Now he did very little of one and none of the other. And the day was beautiful, one of those crisp mornings around seventy-five degrees and no clouds around, just the great open blue. Summer was winding down, and the circus left the locals to enjoy what they claimed as theirs. One of those days where even something like being unemployed didn't matter much. The only thing to do when he felt that good was to start drinking and keep drinking until he felt bad again because it felt morally wrong to feel so good when things were going so poorly.

On the way back to the bar, Hank passed a blonde girl sitting by herself at one of the picnic tables. He pointed her out to Rodney.

"I know," he said. "She's got a nice rack."

Her breasts were large and she wore a low-cut sundress that you couldn't help looking where you knew you shouldn't.

"Go talk to her," Rodney said. "Invite her on the boat."

"I'm married," Hank said.

"I always forget there are people who believe in such weird ideas. I don't see a ring on that finger though," Rodney said.

"I left it at the house since I was going diving."

"Do it for me then."

"I'm not doing it."

Rodney hollered out to the girl, "Hey, are you waiting on someone?"

She smiled and shook her head slightly, but didn't lift her eyes to look who said it.

"Come on, go ask her to hang out. I'll wait for you down by the dinghy."

"Goddamn it, man. You're going to get me in trouble."

"By what I read in the paper a few months ago, you

seem to be doing a damn good job of getting yourself in trouble."

Hank sat across from her. He tried to look her in her eyes, but his eyes kept drifting down. Why else would she where a dress like that, he thought. Her arms were crossed just beneath her big breasts and they rested on her forearms. She had two small scabs on her elbows and what looked like a dozen picked-open mosquito bites on her arms.

Hank looked up and she smiled. She was missing a tooth, one of the canines.

"Why are you sitting alone?" Hank asked.

"I don't know anyone," she said with a strong eastern-European accent. Russian maybe. Hank didn't know.

"What are you doing in Pensacola?" he asked her.

"Do you know where any swing clubs are?" she asked.

"Excuse me?" Hank said.

"I was hoping to find some swinging before I went home."

"Where is home?"

"Lithuania," she said.

"How did you end up in Pensacola?"

She shrugged and smiled, her chin down by her shoulder.

After a short pause, Hank reached out his hand and told her his name.

She shook it with a cold, clammy, limp hand and said her name, but Hank forgot it as soon as she said it.

"You wanna swing?" Hank said. "I know where we can swing."

Her eyes lit up.

"See that boat out there?"

She said yes.

"Let's go."

She hesitated. "You swing on the boat?"

"You bet."

"There is enough room?"

"Of course. Let's go."

Hank downed his beer and grabbed her hand. Hank looked around making sure he didn't recognize any one as he led her by the hand to the docks.

Rodney, Eric, and another couple were already in the dinghy half way out to the boat. Hank and the Lithuanian girl sat at the edge of the dock and dangled their feet just above the water as they watched Rodney and the rest get to the boat and climb aboard. A few minutes went by and Rodney still hadn't come back to get them. Hank tried to keep some conversation, but it was forced and uncomfortable and he couldn't understand most things she said. She had been there about a week, maybe. Hank thought she said something about blue socks. He never found out why she was in Pensacola. Or if she said, he missed it.

After about ten minutes and no sign of Rodney returning, Hank told her to wait.

"I'll swim out there, get the dinghy and pick you up."

"No," she said. "I don't think that is a good idea. I'll just leave."

"It won't take long," Hank said. "Have a couple drinks and I'll bring you right back."

"You have any smoke?" she asked.

Hank pulled out his pack.

She laughed. "No. I want to smoke marijuana."

"I'm sure there is some on the boat."

"Okay," she said. "I go with you, but I don't stay long."

"I've got to leave my wallet here so I can swim. You aren't going to rob me, are you? I don't have any money. I'll show you."

She laughed. "I won't rob you, silly."

"I'll just be a minute." Hank took off his shirt and dove in. Swimming hard, thinking, please don't rob me, please don't rob me. He forgot how hard it was to swim fifty yards.

Before making it to the boat he heard Eric and the others laughing. "That motherfucker swam all the way out here," Eric said.

"Fuck you," Hank said, pulling himself onto the dinghy.

"I was coming back to get you," Rodney said.

"You'll never guess what she asked me." Hank didn't give him time to guess. "She wants to know where the swing clubs are."

"Shut the fuck up," Eric said. "What did you tell her?"

"On the boat. What do you think I said?"

Rodney and the others laughed.

"You ought to have heard the way she said it though. She said, 'I was hoping to find some swing.'"

"No shit, just like that?"

"Just like that. Wait till you hear her."

Hank cranked the outboard on the dinghy and pushed off the boat. She was still waiting. She handed Hank his wallet and shirt.

"You are right. You don't have any money," she said.

Once on the boat, Hank handed out beers and then took out Rodney's dive gear. Rodney anchored the boat in the same spot as yesterday when the squall came through. The anchor wouldn't hold, and he didn't have time to pull it up to move to deeper water, so he cut it away and motored to a better protected inlet and used his back-up anchor. It was a six-hundred-dollar anchor, Rodney said, so he wanted to get it before someone else did.

Hank put on the vest and tank and tossed over the flippers and mask before jumping in. He swam to the mask first and set it on his head, then put the flippers on each foot. Rodney turned up the radio on the boat and Hank could smell the reefer being passed around.

Hank was only down for about five minutes when he spotted the anchor resting in only eleven feet of water and the fish were abundant. Plenty of Sheepshead, a few Black Snappers straying from the nearby docks, and tons of baitfish. If he carried a spear gun he would've had dinner for a week. Hank looked at the air gauge, knowing it started low so he couldn't stay down too much longer than to just get the anchor. He needed an extra rope to attach to the anchor so it would reach to the deck and be easier to pull in. He surfaced and hollered up at Rodney for the rope. Rodney threw him one.

"Wait until you hear what happened," he said.

Hank took the rope and went down again not interested in what Rodney said. He attached the rope to the end of the other rope that was attached to the anchor chain and swam back to the top. Rodney reached up and grabbed the end from him and pulled it up.

Rodney then relayed the story of what happened.

"Actually, I don't know what happened," he said. "She freaked out and swam for it." He was talking about the girl from Lithuania. "We got high and were having a good time. I said we were waiting for a few more girls to come out before we started swinging. She then asked how we are all going to dance on the boat. She was asking about swing dance clubs, dummy. So, I told her we thought she meant swinging as in everyone having sex. She said no, really loud, stood up, and jumped over. Purse and all. I called out to her that I'd take her back. But she just kept swimming. She stopped for a bit and I thought, holy shit, she's gonna drown. But then she kept on going. All the way to shore."

"No shit?"

"No shit."

"I didn't even think about swing dancing," Hank said.

Eric laughed and the other couple, maybe in their fifties or sixties, verified that was exactly how it happened. They met Eric the other night at the bar. They also lived on a sailboat and stopped by Pensacola Beach on their way to Pirates Cove in Josephine, Alabama. They were from New Orleans and were returning from an eighteen-month trip where they sailed to New York and back. They sailed around the Keys and up the coast.

"She just jumped?" Hank asked.

"Yep. She was crazy."

Rodney's girlfriend arrived with some other friends and

she waved them down from the dock.

"I guess I better go get her," Rodney said.

Everyone left. The couple was going back to their boat and Rodney and Eric went to get the girls. Hank went into the galley, made a White Russian, and laid up on the deck pretending it was his boat and that it wasn't the Pensacola coast.

The noise of the dinghy woke Hank from his reverie.

"You got some drinks ready for us?" Rodney said as he stepped onto the boat. He and Eric returned with Rodney's girlfriend, Jayna, and two of her friends.

"What's everyone want?" Hank said.

"I want a Beam and water," Rodney said.

"How about frozen margaritas for the ladies?" Hank said.

The girls said yeah. Eric wanted a beer. Hank took a shot of Jim Beam for himself and handed up five beers for everyone while he made the mixed drinks. They were up on the deck smoking and drinking and Hank turned up the music to drown out their conversation. He was now pretending he was on a crew on a yacht in the Caribbean. Stephen Stills sang through the speakers about sailing to the Southern Islands and failing being so easy to do. Failing was so goddamn easy, Hank thought.

"We're out of ice," Hank said serving up the frozen margaritas.

"Shit. Knew I was forgetting something."

"That's why you're paying me the big bucks, right Captain?"

Rodney laughed.

Hank went back downstairs to get his wallet. He worried for a quick minute about the possibility of Rose getting home early and seeing the mess he left in the kitchen and the un-scooped litter box. He also wondered if he left the porno tape in the VHS player. He took another shot to drown out his worry.

"Everybody cool with your drinks before I go," he said. Everyone said they were.

"I expect everyone to be naked by the time I get back," Hank said. "The least I can get for playing bartender is to see some titties."

Rodney and Eric laughed and the girls not so much.

"You're such a dick when you get drunk," Rodney said.

"I'm not drunk just yet," Hank said and took a beer with him for the dinghy ride back to the beach and the walk for the ice. He liked pulling up to the shore in a dinghy with a beer in hand, no shirt or shoes on, and the salt crusting on his burnt shoulders. It wasn't the alcohol that made him feel that way. Not all of it. He liked the way the tourists watched him getting out of the dinghy, and he imagined them thinking that he lived a carefree, pirate life. For that brief moment, he believed it, too. He could put out of his head that he was a recently fired schoolteacher, unmotivated writer, and a failing husband.

Once back at the boat Rodney followed him downstairs and said, "There's another girl coming out. Things should get interesting."

"What do you mean?"

"Remember that twenty-two-year-old I told you I was seeing?"

"Isabella?"

"She's moved on. This is another one. Well, she's coming out."

"What about Jayna?"

"I'm not worried about Jayna. She knows our arrangement. But this new girl, is so sweet and innocent. I guess we'll find out, huh? Do you mind heading back to the bar and sticking around until she shows up?"

"And how am I going to know if it's her?"

"She's smoking hot. She'll be the best-looking girl in the bar. But I told her to wait at the end of the dock. So, if you see a super-hot chick waiting around the dock, then that's her."

"She have a name?"

He told Hank, but Hank forgot it by the time he got back to the bar.

"You find that anchor?" one of the pre-noon drunks sitting at the bar asked. "I saw him cut it away yesterday. I know where it is."

Hank nodded. "I went down and got it."

"Damn, I was going to tell him I'd get it for him for ten bucks."

"Glad you didn't."

The barmaid asked what Hank wanted. He pointed to one of the beer taps in front of him.

She brought it to him.

"Rodney said to put it on his tab."

"That Rodney, he's a nice fella, isn't he?" the drunk said.

Hank nodded. "He's all right." He said all right, but what he meant to say was alright. Nobody was all right. Plenty of people were alright. Hank liked to think he was one of those people. But lately, he wasn't so sure. He wasn't even so sure he was okay, let alone alright and definitely not all right. He was far from that.

Hank drank another beer before he saw Rodney's new friend arrive. And Rodney was right. She was the most beautiful girl that walked through the bar. She continued on to the dock, and Hank followed behind her.

"Hey, are you looking for Rodney?"

She said she was.

"I'm Hank. I'll be taking you out to the boat."

"Wow. A chauffeur," she said.

"Sure," Hank said.

He shook her hand and she said her name, but Hank was so taken by her lips, he didn't hear what she said.

"How long you and Captain Rodney been hanging out?" Hank asked as they motored out.

"*Captain* Rodney?"

"Yeah, that's how he likes to be referred to when there is more than four people on the boat."

"I didn't know that," she said.

"Oh, so you guys have just started hanging out, huh?"

"I guess so."

Hank smiled.

As they approached, Rodney, Jayna, and Eric were in the water, splashing around. The other two girls sunbathed on the deck.

"You know Jayna?" Hank asked.

She said she didn't and then waved at Rodney. He either didn't see her or ignored her.

"You know why he calls it the *Sure Thang*, don't you?" Hank asked her as she climbed up the ladder.

"He told me," she said, rolling her eyes.

Hank laughed.

He then asked her what she wanted to drink.

"Just a beer," she said.

"Everyone else has already been drinking tequila," he said.

She said okay. Hank made her a strong margarita on the rocks. She said it was too strong.

"It's just right," Hank said.

Rodney pulled himself from the water onto the boat and sat next to Twenty-Two-Year-Old. Hank stepped from the galley and threw Rodney a towel before handing him a can of beer and throwing another one in the water to Eric. The other girls, sunbathing, said they were good. Jayna climbed the ladder.

"About to get good," Hank said.

Rodney smiled.

Jayna introduced herself to the other girl.

"So, this is the twenty-two-year-old you've been going on about?" Jayna said to Rodney.

"Is that what you call me when I'm not around?" Twenty-Two-Year-Old said.

"He has a hard time remembering names," Jayna said.

She sat on the other side of Rodney. Rodney smiled at Hank. Hank sat in the captain's chair, his feet propped up on the steering wheel as he sipped his beer. He shook his head in astonishment or confusion.

"Is that right?" Twenty-Two-Year-Old said.

"I think it took him about two weeks to learn mine," Jayna said.

"I'm sorry. Are you two?" Twenty-Two-Year-Old motioned between them. "Are you two?"

"A couple?" Jayna finished the question for her.

Rodney laughed. Hank took another sip. Eric yelled for the other girls to jump in. One did. The other stayed on the deck with her too-big sunglasses blocking out the world.

"That's a good question. What are we, Rodney?" Jayna asked.

"I don't like labels," he said.

"I'm kidding," Jayna said. "We are just friends. Ain't that right?"

He nodded. "Let's swim." He dove overboard.

Jayna went to the deck with her friend. Twenty-Two-Year-Old took off her shirt and shorts and revealed a better body than Hank imagined. Jayna and her friend noticed too because they were looking at her as well. Hank joined Jayna and the other girl on the deck.

"Finished swimming?" he said.

"For now," she said.

"Need a drink?"

"I'm good."

Too-Big Glasses didn't acknowledge he spoke.

Hank downed his beer and climbed the main mast. The boat was a ketch and the spreaders of the main mast were about at the height of the top of the mizzen mast. It was taller than Jimmy's old sloop that Hank used to jump from. Hank never jumped from the new boat.

"Watch this motherfucker," Rodney said from down below. Everyone looked up and hooted and hollered.

Hank stood on the spreaders for a second and looked out at one of the most beautiful beaches he ever saw, a place where thousands came on vacation, yet others were lucky enough to call home. The difference being that the tourists often times didn't see what the locals did, the county outside of the beach. The horrible education system, the low-paying jobs, the crime, the drugs. When the majority of the people worked in the service industry, poverty became an endless cycle that only a few lucky ones could break. Hank nearly did, but after his arrest, he wasn't so sure he ever stood a chance.

Hank leapt and hit the water. He sunk deep and swam until his lungs burned. He wanted to stay down there. He wasn't ready to come up and wasn't sure if he ever would be ready, but as his lungs neared explosion he burst through the surface.

Everyone clapped for his leap and he shouted, "How come no one is naked yet?"

Eric and the other girl were hanging onto an inner tube that was tied to the side of the boat and Eric said, "I'm bout, too."

The girl with him said he wouldn't.

"Do it," Rodney said and Eric pulled off his shorts and held them in the air. The girls on the deck sat up to get a better look and cheered and clapped. Rodney hooted. Twenty-Two-Year-Old looked a bit concerned.

"You're next," Hank said swimming up next to her and Rodney.

"I don't think so," she said.

"Don't listen to Hank. He's already drank too much."

The girl with Eric took off her bottoms, too. Everyone cheered again, except for Twenty-Two-Year-Old. She seemed to get more worried.

"Let's see them titties," Eric said and reached for the girl's top. She was able to get away from him and pushed off the inner tube and swam out a ways and then dove under, her white ass breaking the surface like a Beluga whale. Everyone cheered, sounding like school children on a field trip to Sea World. When she resurfaced she was covered again.

Hank booed. She said, "I don't see you getting naked?"

Jayna shouted down from the boat, "Come on, Hank. Let's see what you've got."

"You get me a beer and jump in, I'll get naked," Hank said.

Jayna went below deck and came back with an armful of beers and threw them into the water. Rodney asked her to toss in the boogie board as well. She did and then her and the other girl dove in.

"The party begins," Rodney said. "You said you would get naked, Hank. Get naked."

"You sound a bit excited about that," Jayna said to him.

She and the other girl were hanging onto the inner tube also. Twenty-Two-Year-Old and Hank were the only ones treading water. Treading water was nothing new for Hank Ackerman.

"It wouldn't be the first time I've seen him naked. Me and him have shared some intimate moments in my old boat. Specially, up in that V-birth," Rodney said.

Hank laughed. "The *Sure Thang* doesn't just work on women, you know."

Jayna shook her head. Twenty-Two-Year-Old looked like she believed them.

"You getting naked or what?" Jayna said to Hank.

"You first."

Her top came off without hesitation. She even lifted out of the water so Hank could see those great breasts. The sun caught the water drips just right as they gleamed off her brown nipples.

She put her top on the inner tube, swam over to Rodney, and wrapped her arms around his waist from behind, her breasts squishing on his back, but she kept her eyes on Hank, smiling. She knew he liked what he saw.

Twenty-Two-Year-Old said, "Seriously, you're not his girlfriend?"

Rodney laughed. "There's enough for two of you," he said. Jayna laughed. Twenty-Two-Year-Old didn't seem to find that funny. She swam to the boat.

"Some people haven't broken the monogamy brainwash yet," Rodney said and Jayna bit his neck.

Hank followed Twenty-Two-Year-Old to the boat.

"Can you take me back to shore? I didn't know he had

a girlfriend."

"Of course," Hank said.

Hank dropped Twenty-Two-Year-Old off and went to the bar and ordered another beer on Rodney's tab. He asked the barmaid what time it was. She told him. Shit. He should've been home. He borrowed a quarter from someone at the bar and called the house from the payphone. He would leave a message for Rose, explaining he was making money and he may be a bit late.

Instead she answered.

"Hey, Babe. Didn't think you would be home already…I'm working…Out on Rodney's boat. He needed help finding an anchor…Twenty-five dollars…He's giving me fifty bucks to play bartender for five hours…I don't know. Some of his friends…Another hour, at the most…I'm not drunk…Two beers is all…What's so important that I have to come home right now? Well, I can't…Just tell me… You sure you can't just tell me…? Okay. See you in a bit. Love you."

Recently, she stopped saying "love you" back to him and she turned to offer her cheek instead of lips when he kissed her goodbye.

It was three more hours before Hank got home. When he went back to the boat he knew Rodney was getting too drunk to ever pay him, but knowing him for so long, he knew where Rodney kept his cash. There was one hundred and twenty dollars in the drawer in the V-birth. Hank thought of taking it all, but once it was in his pocket he felt a little wrong for doing so and only took ninety-five. The extra five he owed for the ice and then ten more for having to write his own paycheck. He didn't know how it took three more hours to leave, but he made another batch of margaritas and a couple of beer bottles broke in the cockpit, which he swept, and a short-lived dance party took place downstairs. Eric fell down the companionway and scraped his shin. One of the girls pretended to be sober and administered first aid, while the rest of them laughed. Rodney walked out of the bathroom naked and swung his dick back and forth. Somebody threw up. Not because he walked out naked, but later. A lot of pot was smoked. Rodney's speech started slurring pretty bad and he was spitting when he talked. One of the girls, not the one who did first aid and not Jayna, went to sleep in the V-birth. Rodney argued with Eric that he should go join her. They went back and forth before Eric finally did. And somehow, Rodney got Hank back to shore with the dinghy.

Hank pulled up to the house, took a deep breath, and walked inside. Rose was in the kitchen.

"So," Hank said. "What was so important that you had to wait to tell me in person?"

He kissed her on the cheek and poured a glass of water. He looked at her and she was standing over the sink crying.

"Is it that bad?"

She looked at him with red, wet eyes.

"I'm pregnant," she said.

Hank grabbed onto the countertop to stop the room from spinning.

"What?" he asked.

"I'm pregnant," she said again and turned away crying.

"You sure?"

"I took two tests. I left them in the bathroom if you want to see."

"I believe you, but why are you crying?" he asked.

She started laughing through her sobs. "How the hell are we going to raise a child? You don't even have a job."

Hank hugged her from behind. "I don't know," he said. "But we'll manage. People worse off than us manage."

"That's not very comforting," she said.

"What do you want me to say?"

"I don't know."

"What are you saying?"

"I don't know. I'm going to bed. You're drunk."

Hank tried to hug her, but she pulled away.

"I'm going to bed, Hank. Some of us have to work in the morning."

She went to bed. Hank filled a glass of water from the faucet and drank the entire pint in three gulps. He walked outside and took his bicycle from the garage to go for a ride.

He grabbed a beer at the gas station down the road and rode to the bay behind the Bayfront Auditorium. People fished under the yellow lights. Hank sat on a bench looking out across the bay at the boat lights shimmering in the water.

He thought about how he grew up and knew he didn't want to raise a child like that. He took a pull from the can and held it out and looked at it before pouring the rest of the beer out.

He got back on his bike and rode around a bit more. He rode hard, the wind making his eyes water. Tears streaked down his cheeks as he peddled around the city watching people sit outside and eat and drink and laugh. He saw the homeless men and women gathered in Plaza Ferdinand. He heard music coming from one of the bars that looked like it belonged in New Orleans with filigree iron balconies. The car lights that passed by him brightened the Mardi Gras beads hanging in the trees.

At least now, Rose might not leave him like she planned, he thought.

Fly, Brother, Fly!

Braden drove his yellow convertible Corvette on the far eastside of town along the scenic highway overlooking a forty-foot bluff that ran parallel to the bay. The car had only nine thousand miles on it. A gift from his step-father for getting into law school.

He didn't have a particular destination in mind, only the town of Sullivan. At twenty-two years of age, his life never strayed from the plan. That was the problem.

He attended college directly out of high school, graduated at the top of his class, and was accepted into the same law-school his step-father attended. He recently married his high-school sweetheart when he found out she was pregnant. After law-school, he would see his name on his step-father's law firm.

Braden merged off the Interstate 10 and headed north on HWY 29 and stopped just before the Florida-Alabama state line in the quiet, swampy, nearly-forgotten town of Sullivan. A town once known for lumber, but now making headlines for crystal meth, dog fights, and bingo parlor robberies. A town where making good money meant being able to afford a case of Busch beer on payday and people fished and hunted and dreamed, but the dreams mostly stayed dreams, rarely becoming a reality. It never seemed to grow out of its post-Civil War heyday as a lumber mill and turpentine town. But once the lumber industry dwindled, the rich moved on to other ventures in other cities and the workers were left with nothing but a half-hearted will to survive.

Braden was amazed that with a quick drive he could enter into what felt like a time machine and visit a place where responsibility meant living at the same address for more than a year instead of how diversified you kept a portfolio. Nearly fifty miles from the city he was born in, he turned off the highway, and hidden deep into the woods near a fishing camp on the Escambia River, sat a bar, secluded enough to easily be missed.

He saw a sign with the words "Warm Beer and Lousy Food" and followed the arrow painted under the words onto a gravel path lined with second-growth slash pine and scrub oak that led to an empty oyster shell parking lot and an unpainted wooden house. A historic marker said the house was built in 1892 and stood on an old mill site. The house, years ago converted into a tavern, was shaded beneath the pines that were replanted about fifty years ago and survived six floods and eleven hurricanes, and if the trees had eyes would've witnessed two lynchings during the start of the Jim Crow laws. One tree, that looked much older than any he ever saw, was riddled with bullet holes that locals claimed were from when the law attempted to capture Railroad Bill in 1895. Railroad Bill was the African-American train robber and his ghost was said to still haunt the tracks. Next to the tavern, a dock hung out over the shallow grassy water.

Braden walked to the water, slapped mosquitoes from his neck and brushed love bugs from his face. Crickets and toads sang the song of the wilderness. His shirt stuck to his back from the sweat. He loosened his tie, but it didn't offer any relief. He contemplated venturing onto the unsteady dock but decided against it.

Inside the tavern, an old man wearing a tattered captain's hat was hunched over an unfrosted mug at the corner of the mahogany bar. Chairs were stacked on the tables and water streaks shone on the linoleum floor. The only sound came from the slurping of the old man as he sipped the froth of a freshly poured beer, and the only bit of light besides the door that Braden still held open came from the red light hanging over the pool table. He took a few seconds to adjust his eyes to the darkness. A sign on the wall behind the bar read, "Free beer tomorrow." Three dart boards lined the back wall. The old man continued slurping, not lifting the mug from the bar and paying no mind to Braden standing in the doorway scanning the place while dust particles swirled in the thick ray of sunlight surrounding him.

He sat at the opposite end of the bar of the old man. The old man turned and acknowledged him with a slight nod. The man had an impossible number of wrinkles around his eyes. His skin drooped from his cheeks like a bull dog. Gray whiskers poked out from his oversized ears. The pores on his red, puffed nose looked open enough to stick a toothpick in. The old man took off his hat, set it on the bar, and scratched at the speckled, brown-crusted spots on his bald head before replacing the cap back on his head.

"How do I get a drink?" Braden asked.

The old man looked into his mug, studied what was in it, lifted it off the bar and downed half, his throat just sort of opening up and allowing the beer to flow down, not necessarily using his throat muscles to swallow. He lifted his heavy eyes briefly to Braden's, but didn't say anything. He lowered them again and stared at nothing. After a minute, he looked back up and stared at Braden's left hand.

"Married, huh?" The words barely audible.

"What was that?" Braden said.

"Noticed you're married."

"Yeah," Braden said. "I am. You're not the bartender, are ya?"

"I'm not." The old man looked back into his mug.

Braden shouted out, "Hello?"

The white-haired barkeep popped his head out from the door behind the bar. He pulled his head back before he spoke. "Be out in a minute," he said. Then, "Keep my customer entertained, would ya, Merle?"

Braden looked down at the old man and around at the rest of the room. He noticed the jukebox in the corner and searched his pockets for change.

"Don't you dare," Merle said.

"Excuse me?"

"Don't even think of playing any music at this time of day."

Braden laughed. "Might cheer this place up," he said. Braden stood up and went to the jukebox. The old man slowly stood and followed him, dragging his feet. He could barely make it a couple of steps without having to hold onto the nearest table.

"You want to pick something?" Braden asked him. "You pick something. Then I will. My treat."

The old man didn't answer and stood glaring down at

the jukebox, holding on to the table with his shaky arms.

"All right," Braden said. "Hope you like what I pick. I gave you a chance." Braden put his money in, scanned the options, and chose two songs by Creedence Clearwater Revival. "Everyone likes CCR, right?"

The old man said, "I like them just fine." But as soon as the music started the old man reached down and unplugged the machine and worked his way back to the bar.

Braden laughed. "I'll be damned," he said. "If you weren't so old, I might've kicked your ass for that."

"You could've tried," Merle grunted.

The bartender, now behind the bar, witnessed what happened, and he dried his hands on a rag, tossed it over his shoulder, and said, "You behaving, Merle?"

Merle nodded.

Although white as could be, the bartender still maintained a good head of hair and his unnaturally blue eyes shined from under bushy eyebrows that were of the same white color. His skin was wrinkled, but with a bit more elasticity than poor Merle's. He wore a black apron over black trousers and a black collared shirt.

"Sorry about the wait. People don't usually come in this early."

Braden motioned with his head over toward Merle.

"Except Merle," the barkeep said.

Merle grunted.

"What'll ya have?"

"A beer'll be fine."

"Any particular?"

"A cold one, preferably."

"Did you read the sign? I'll see what I got."

"Speaking of the sign, this place have a name?"

The barkeep poured him a pint, setting it down on a paper napkin on the long wooden bar and said, "Some people still call it Sally's Cricket Shack, but that's not really the name. Just a name that's kind of grown on it, you know?"

"Why do they call it Sally's Cricket Shack?"

"Sally is a bartender here and she sells crickets."

"Okay."

"You mind if I just finish up in the back? It'll be just a minute."

"That's fine. Go right ahead."

The bartender did.

"Married," Merle mumbled.

"We've determined this. Yes, I'm married." Braden took a long drink. "If you don't mind, I'm not really interested in talking about my marriage."

"Sometimes it's best," Merle said with phlegm drowning out the last word. He coughed. "That's what she used to tell me."

Braden ignored him, but Merle continued staring at him.

"Fine. I'll play along," Braden said. "Who? Your wife? She used to tell you that?"

Merle nodded. "She did. Always wanted to talk. Could never just sit and enjoy the quiet."

"Interesting," Braden said.

They sat next to each other in silence, each taking a sip at different times, but sometimes they coincided because

Merle kept a little quicker rhythm. Braden rubbed his thumb over his wedding band, and the old man noticed him doing that.

"I used to do that when the marriage was still new," Merle said. Braden didn't say anything but glanced at the old man's left hand to see if he was wearing a band as well. He was.

Some time passed allowing Braden and the old man to finish their drinks quietly. The barkeep came out and saw the two patiently awaiting another beer.

While pouring the drinks he said, "So, who's your friend, Merle?"

"Don't know if he's my friend." Merle coughed again, clearing the phlegm from his throat. It could have been mistaken as a laugh.

The barkeep set the beers in front of them and said, "What's your name, stranger?"

"Braden. Braden Anders." He stuck out his hand. The barkeep shook it. He glared at Merle. Merle looked into his beer. "I'm Braden," he said again and extended his hand to Merle this time.

"I heard ya," Merle said.

Braden picked up his beer and took two big drinks.

"He's married," Merle said. The barkeep smiled at Merle.

"That's right," Braden said. "Sure am."

After a brief silence, the barkeep said, "If you two kids can stay out of trouble, I'm just going to clean the bathrooms real quick." Neither Braden nor the old man responded.

Braden turned on his stool, leaning back with elbows up on the bar and looked at the empty room. Large wooden beams ran across the twelve-foot ceilings. Merle turned and stood in the same manner as Braden. Braden looked at him but said nothing. Merle picked up his mug and took a sip and peered over the rim of his mug at Braden. "Nice place. Used to be a house?" Braden asked.

Merle didn't respond.

"Want to throw a game of darts?" Braden said.

"No." Merle turned back around. Braden did the same. Merle lifted his eyes to Braden, who could see it out of the corner of his eyes but kept his eyes trained on the turned off TV.

"Something bothering you, old man?"

"Nope."

"You keep looking up like you'd like to say something."

Merle looked at him. His eyelids drooped down over the tops of his eyes giving him a slant-eye gaze. His gray eyes foggy, cataracts maybe. "Just waiting on you," he said.

"To do what?" Braden said.

The old man took another swig leaving just a swallow in the bottom of the mug. The barkeep poked his head out from the bathroom and shouted, "Bout ready for another?" Merle lifted his mug. The barkeep came back behind the bar.

"So, Braden, what's brought you here?" He set down the drinks.

"Visiting from St. Louis," Braden replied and took a sip.

"Why the hell did you come to Sullivan? Pensacola is about fifty miles south of here."

"Yeah, I know. I didn't come for the beach. I came to find my old man. He grew up around here. Hank Ackerman. Ever hear of him?"

Merle kept his head down but lifted his eyes at the barkeep. The barkeep smiled at him.

"Ackerman?" the barkeep said. "Yeah. I heard of him. Knew his daddy and his brother, too."

"He still come around?" Braden asked.

"No son. The old man died years ago. Teddy, the brother, not too long ago. But Hank, hell, ain't nobody seen Hank. Last we heard, he got into some trouble down in Pensacola and run off. No telling what ol' Hank is doing. He was the only one ever worth a shit, too. Just didn't seem to be able to break free of this place."

"Momma told me not to bother looking for him. Said he was no good. But I'd like to know where I come from, you know?"

"Hell, son. Sometimes it's better not to."

"Maybe so."

"What do you do for work?"

"Heading to law school."

"How about your wife?" Merle said entering the conversation.

Braden looked over at him. "She's a nurse."

The barkeep then walked from behind the bar and began taking the chairs down. Braden looked at the old man who still stared down into his mug, running his finger, the one with the wedding band, around the rim.

"So, you're married," Braden said followed by a

smart-ass grin.

"Not anymore," Merle managed, though it sounded as if the phlegm built up again.

"She passed? I apologize."

Merle shook his head no. "I don't think so."

"What does that mean?"

"Who knows?"

"You don't have to talk about it."

Merle slowly sat up straight, exhaled deeply and cleared the phlegm from his throat. "I'll tell ya, if you want." He looked over at Braden who was now a bit hunched over. "Hey, old man," Merle said to the barkeep, "How bout you get me and my friend here some good stuff?" Braden looked over at Merle and smirked. The wrinkles around Merle's deep, clouded eyes smiled.

The barkeep came back around the bar and set out three shot glasses and a bottle of Jameson's Irish whiskey. He poured them each a drink. The three of them held up the glasses, nodded, and drank. Braden shivered a bit. The other two looked as if it were only water.

"Seriously, I don't want to pry," Braden said.

The barkeep reached across the bar and patted Merle on the shoulder.

"Me and Maude met back in 1954. We had a good time back then. Was never concerned about whether tomorrow ever came."

"It's good being young, eh Braden?" the barkeep added.

Braden looked down into his mug. "Wouldn't know."

Merle and the barkeep looked at each other. The barkeep

shrugged.

"Anyway," Merle continued, "I was twenty-two, maybe. I don't remember, maybe twenty-three. Not twenty-five yet though, I don't think. I had already been married once before. That one was a mistake. I had just come back from Korea. And I was done with the military. It wasn't for me, ya know." He sipped his whiskey.

"Yeah, wish I hadn't ever been," the barkeep added. "I went to Vietnam in sixty-six. Did four years and came home. Enough for me, too."

"My dad served," Braden said. "Well, my step-dad. I never had to." There was a short silence.

"I started working on a charter boat down in Gulf Shores," Merle said. "Taking rich folks fishing. Maude wanted to go to college, be a teacher. Elementary school. Her parents weren't thrilled with her running around with a fisherman twelve years older than she was. But she couldn't get enough of old Merle." Merle started laughing and that laugh turned into a cough.

"Then what happened?" the barkeep said. He took a sip from the whiskey. Braden followed. The barkeep topped off the drinks. Braden felt that the barkeep had heard this story before.

"Well, with Vietnam going on, I was concerned with getting drafted back in. I thought if that was to happen I'd lose Maude. Maude had just finished college, but never took a job as a teacher. She started getting big into that hippy shit and I liked the drugs."

"I was one, too. After the war." They laughed a bit

before Merle started again.

"So, me and the captain of the boat I worked on started talking about getting the hell out of town. He said he was going to sell his charter boat and buy a sailboat. He heard he could make good money smuggling marijuana from Central America. He did it and bought a thirty-eight-foot sailboat. It could sleep six people comfortably. He called it the *Green Rocket*. It was a beauty." He cleared his throat and took a deep breath to get through the rest of what he wanted to say. "We were going to a place we had heard was like Eden, unlike anything we ever saw. Costa Rica. Back then, it wasn't like it is today. It was uncharted territory. Maude was all about it, too. I didn't believe she had it in her. I thought it was just the hippy talk, you know, tune in and drop out, but she was serious. We still hadn't gotten married yet, and she was still kind of living off her parents. But she was willing to give it up. She wasn't looking for the American Dream. Wasn't quite ready to throw her fishing line in the main stream just yet. She was something. Crazy girl. And beautiful. Never knew a more beautiful girl. Inside and out. Pure as the devil. So we did it. We hopped ship and sailed away."

"Just showed how much you were in love," the barkeep said.

Merle nodded, finished off the whiskey and the barkeep refilled it.

"That's great," Braden said. "Just chucked everything and went for it, huh? Just like that. No regrets, no worries?"

"You're just getting a piece of this guy today," the barkeep said. "This man has got some of the best stories around.

Just look at him. Everything about him says adventure."

Merle smiled, acknowledging the compliment. "Wish it hadn't taken me so long to learn the lessons from those adventures."

The barkeep lifted his shot glass. Merle and Braden did the same and each took a sip. The barkeep topped them off.

"Let me tell you about this place," Merle said. "First of all, we sailed through the Panama Canal. We heard the Caribbean side of Costa Rica wasn't the place to go. Heard it was a bit more dangerous. Creeping with pirates and whatnot. Sailing the Canal in itself is an adventure when you think of its history. You know what it took to build that thing?"

Braden said he didn't. The barkeep nodded that he did.

Merle continued, "It took thirty-four years to finish and cost the U.S. three hundred and fifty million dollars. More than anything built by our government at that time. Between us and the French, it was something like six hundred and fifty million dollars. A lot of money to create a banana republic, huh? Eighty thousand people worked on that thing. Thirty thousand of them died. But you don't see any memorials for them, do ya? Nothing. Died like goddamned slaves."

"It's sad," the barkeep said. Braden nodded in agreement. "All for some goddamn bananas and coffee."

"But for all the shit that went into building it, I got to say, cruising along it was a thing of beauty. Out there, far from home, we didn't even mention the bullshit that had been taking place back home. It was like it never existed. And when we sailed into Costa Rica, I can't even describe what it looked like. Today, their economy runs off tourism. Back then, coffee and bananas. Only a handful of other expats living there. And they were happy to share their little piece of paradise. No one thought it could ever get too crowded. No one ever imagined it would turn into resort towns. It was a new kind of society. They even did away with the Army there in 1946 or '48. It was what the hippies dreamed of. But these people lived it. They had a lifestyle I only saw in bad movies at the time. But over there it was something pure and raw and real. Surfing. You ever surf, Braden?"

Braden shook his head. "Haven't done a lot of things," he said.

"You should try it."

"Don't really have the time."

"Time is a bitch, isn't it?"

"I want to hear the end of the story," the barkeep said.

"You know how it ends. But anyway, we were the only ones with a boat at this place we were at and we started taking people surfing. Places they couldn't reach by foot. We found a place with a giant rock just sitting out in the middle of the water. I think they call it Witch's Rock now. Ever heard of it?"

Braden turned his lips down in a frown and shook his head no.

"Phenomenal place. I mean this is what the kids back in the States wanted but was too chicken-shit to really search for. They looked for it in LSD and other bullshit. Hell, I did too. But with drugs, it wasn't real. It was out there. In the world. It wasn't just some made-up fantasy. And these other people figured it out. I'm sure glad we did, too. I mean, with all the shit going on at home, with war, protests, and politics and what-have-you, this place didn't even have a military. Can you believe that? A country with no army? Have you ever heard of such a thing? Ain't that something?"

"That's crazy," Braden said. "Why'd you ever come back here?"

The barkeep looked down at Merle.

"I'm sorry," Braden said. "Keep telling us about Costa Rica."

The old man drank his whiskey. The barkeep poured another.

"I'll cut to the chase," Merle said. "Maude began to miss home. We heard the war was over and she hadn't talked to anyone from home in over nine years. Hell, she didn't even know if her parents were still alive. She missed her little brother graduate from high school. I didn't want to go back. We had a big fight about it. I was about to let her leave on her own when she told me the real reason. She was pregnant. So in '74 we flew home. Left the captain there. He married a local Tica and was happy. Me and Maude had gotten married while we were over there. One of the expats was an ordained minister and did the ceremony. But, man, I wasn't ready for no damn kid. Not in this fucked-up world I told her. When we got home she didn't tell anyone she was pregnant and I took her to a doctor who took care of it for us. She wasn't ever the same after that. I guess I wasn't either. We weren't the same. Life wasn't the same."

"Damn," Braden said. And waited for more. "Hate to hear that."

"Shit. Her parents tried to act like we were still kids. I was a forty-two-year-old man and she was thirty and they wanted us to move in with them until she could find a teaching job. Her dad said he knew someone who could get me a job with the city. And they wanted us to have a real wedding. Maude started believing all the shit we tried so hard to escape. We got married in a church. They cut my hair and my beard and put me in a tux and converted me to a damn Baptist. In Costa Rica, life just crept by. It felt like a day was a year. After we got back it was just a whirlwind. Years flew by. I wasn't happy. She pretended to be. She even quit drinking, started going to church and all that other bullshit. I started spending less and less time with her and more and more time at the bars, and one day I was walking along some docks when I saw a sailboat just like the one we sailed over in and it was cheap. Something like three-thousand dollars. Needed some work, but had a motor and sails and it floated. I was saving up for a house to get us out of her parents' place, but I thought if I bought this boat she would remember what a beautiful life we had back in Costa Rica and maybe want to go back to it. So, I bought the thing and even had the name painted on there – the *Green Rocket II*. I figured that Eden was such a green and lovely place that was so far out of this world only a rocket ship could get us there. I thought she would be thrilled. Not quite."

They all chuckled a bit.

"Excuse me fellas. I don't want to cut you off, but I gotta piss," Braden said. He looked at his watch – two-thirty. Time was going quickly in that little bar. He took a piss, looked in the mirror and tried to focus his eyes. He washed his hands and his face. Merle and the barkeep watched him as he walked back.

"You all right?" the barkeep asked him.

"Another drink and Merle finishes the story and then I got to get out of here," he said. "I'm getting a bit drunk."

"Ain't no more story," Merle said.

"You never even answered the question though."

The barkeep looked at Merle. Merle shrugged his shoulders and hunched back over the bar. He didn't look like the same proud sailor who was telling the story of romantic adventures a few minutes ago. Instead, he returned back into the frail-bodied old man drinking alone at a bar.

"You said you weren't married anymore and not sure if she passed, but you still wear the ring?"

"When we got married, I said it was forever and goddamn it, I meant it," Merle said.

They all sat in silence as Braden drank his last drink.

"How long has it been since you've seen her?" Braden said.

Merle thought for a moment. "Twenty years, maybe. Last I saw, she was married, had two kids, and was an elementary school teacher."

"Did you ever go back to Costa Rica?"

"I did."

"She didn't go with you?"

"She didn't."

"You came back for her?"

Merle nodded. "I was too late."

"But you lived down in Gulf Shores. What brought you back up here? To Sullivan?"

"This is home. And I couldn't stand it if I ran into her again, so I moved back up here to finish out my days where I started."

"Hate to hear that."

"It's not too late for you though."

Braden nodded, but didn't move.

"Fly, brother, fly! What the hell are you waiting for?"

Braden stood longer, looking onto the wall beyond Merle. He felt surprisingly sober.

"You good?" the barkeep asked. "Can I get you some water?"

"I'll take a water to go." He left a fifty for the barkeep.

"Too much, my friend," the barkeep said.

Braden waved the change away. The barkeep nodded, and the old man saluted.

Braden opened the heavy door and let in the brightness that reflected off the oyster shells in the parking lot. He squinted as he walked over to his car, looking at his watch once more. His wife was waiting for him at the hotel in Pensacola. She would know he was drunk. She would yell at him for drinking and driving when he has a kid on the way. He'd try to explain, but she would start crying and he'd go for a walk and hope the argument would blow over by the time he returned. He would like to tell her that he loved her and he appreciated their life, but deep down, he knew something was missing. He'd think about Merle's story and tell himself how lucky he was to have that special someone, but he knew, every now and then, that something would find its way back to him, and he didn't know any other way to get it out. He hoped that finding his father would've filled some of that missing piece. He opened his car door, but before stepping in he stared out at a boy fishing from a canoe in the river that emptied to the bay and continued to the Gulf of Mexico and continued further to anywhere and everywhere.

Saga of Milt Andrews

The first day of a twenty-five-year sentence for triple manslaughter, aggravated assault, and numerous other charges. He didn't want to harm others. That was his old self. He was reformed now. He gave his life to Jesus only minutes before the tragedy.

Milt Andrews thought he had been at rock bottom before, but this time he burrowed to new depths. It was his third time being fired from a construction job for getting too drunk on his lunch break. The first time, he fell off the roof, breaking a collarbone and his left arm. The second time, he dropped a bucket of hot tar, and it splashed on one of the new guys, scalding his leg with third-degree burns. The last time, though, was it. He was taking a piss from above, something he was warned about numerous times, when the foreman walked underneath without a hard hat on and took the warm, yellow liquid on his bald head. Milt tried to argue that the foreman should have been wearing his hat.

Milt decided not to go directly home after being fired. Peg would leave for sure this time. She was a waitress, putting in nearly fifty hours a week at the Waffle Stop and she told him before that she couldn't be with a man who couldn't hold a job. She was the one that made him go groveling, begging to get his job back every time he was fired. He would convince his boss he quit drinking, but after a few weeks on the job he was back at it. It was hard to quit when everyone else was passing around beers. But the others knew when to stop or at least stay functional. Milt would get four or five beers in him and then start in on the whiskey.

At just a minute past noon, Milt pulled up to his favorite watering hole, Sally's Cricket Shack. A few cars were parked out front as were two Harley Davidson Fat Boys that Milt recognized. When he entered the poorly lit cave, Rhonda was serving drinks. Butterchurn and Skeet and Skeet's girl Kathy were bellied-up to the bar. Applesauce was in the corner pounding away at a Dolly Parton pinball machine with his pit-bull, What's-the-Point, sitting by his side. Butterchurn and Skeet laughed when they saw Milt enter.

"It ain't raining, Milt. What are you doing here so early?" Rhonda said as Milt took his place at the bar. You could tell Rhonda was a looker in her days. She still wore miniskirts and fishnet stockings and she dyed her hair in different colors. This day she had blue streaks running through, but some gray still showed at the roots.

Milt hung his head.

"You fired again?" Skeet said. Kathy slapped him on the arm. Skeet laughed and his belly shook. "What?" he said. "Oh shit. You are, aren'tcha?"

Milt nodded.

"Damn, Milt. You drunk again?" Rhonda asked.

Milt shook his head. "Notch yet," he said.

"What the hell happened?" Skeet asked.

"Wait. Can't this man have a drink first," Kathy said. She stood up and put her arm across his shoulders. "It's alright, baby." Milt always liked the way Kathy's bright red hair smelled.

"It's not alright," he said. "Not this time."

Rhonda drew him a beer.

"It's gonna take more than that," he said.

"The man wants a drink, get him a drink," Skeet said and laughed.

"Shut up, wouldja?" Kathy said to him.

"No, I won't. He's my buddy, I'ma take care of him." Then he turned to Rhonda. "Get him a shot of the good stuff, and me too. Want one, Butter? You, Applesauce?"

Applesauce declined and kept pounding away at the pinball machine.

Rhonda poured four shots. They were gone just as quick as she poured them.

"Why don't we throw some darts?" Skeet suggested.

"You go ahead," Milt said. Butterchurn and Skeet went to the dart board. Kathy stayed with Milt and Rhonda at the bar.

"It's Peggy, isn't it, hun?" Kathy said. "Is that what's got you worried?"

Milt nodded. He looked up at Rhonda. She poured him another drink. He nursed that one.

"You think she'll mean it this time?" Rhonda asked. She looked at Kathy. Kathy nodded, but not so Milt could see.

"Yeah, it's over. I'm just gonna wait till she's gone to work and then get my stuff and go to a hotel or something." He took another sip. "I probably got enough money for a couple days."

"You know, we've got that RV out back our house you can stay in for a bit. Save some money," Rhonda said. "Ain't got A/C, but we can run some fans in there. And I bet

Butter'll let you clean some pools or something for some extra cash until you get back on your feet."

Milt shook his head and downed his drink. "I'll be fine." He threw a twenty on the bar. "Do you mind?" he asked grabbing the neck of the three-quarter full bottle of whiskey.

"Keep your money, Milt," Rhonda said. "We got this one."

"Thank you."

She grabbed his other hand and squeezed it and said, "I'll try to talk to her, if you'd like."

He nodded. "I'd sure appreciate it."

Kathy gave him a good, long hug and said, "We love you, Milt. Be safe."

He left without saying bye to the guys.

Outside, he unscrewed the cap and tossed it in the oyster shell lot, took a strong pull, his Adam's apple moving up and down a few times, and began walking, not knowing where to. He walked behind the bar into the woods where a trail led to a small creek that eventually fed into the bay down in Pensacola.

He sat down on the creek's edge and drank and drank and drank as the sun sailed across the sky on its way to the western horizon, creating hues of purple and orange until the bottle was nearly empty and he was drunk. He threw the bottle into the creek. He was drunk enough now to not notice the mosquitoes biting on his neck and arms.

He stood up, swayed backward, regained his footing, took a step forward, paused to gain his footing again, and then as he lost all sense of balance, he reached for a branch that he thought was much closer than it was and fell onto his back. His head and left shoulder hit the water's edge, but his nose and mouth remained out of the water so he allowed himself to lay there a while and fell asleep.

Butterchurn shook him awake.

"Damn, Milt, you drunker than horse shit." He helped him up and held him steady.

"A man can't sleep?"

"Yeah, you can sleep. Not in the water though."

"Well, I'm awake now, damn it. And ain't got no place to go."

Butterchurn walked behind Milt to make sure he didn't fall over again. He lost his footing twice on the mossy ground but never took a true spill. The bar was more crowded now. Skeet and Kathy had left, but Applesauce was still pounding on the pinball. People didn't say anything to Milt as he walked in, but their eyes were on him. His hair was disheveled and wet, and his shirt was muddy. He had a few cuts on his arms and neck from falling on the briars, sticks, and whatever else was down there. He didn't pay any attention to the gawkers. He stumbled to the bar and took a seat. Rhonda brought him water.

"What the hell I want with this? Give me a drink," he slurred.

Rhonda looked at Butterchurn.

"That ain't such a good idea there, Milt," Butterchurn said.

"You ain't gonna give me a drink, Rhonda?" And then to Butterchurn, "You my friend?"

"Of course."

"Then give me a fucking drink."

Rhonda walked to the other side of the bar to tend to the other customers. Milt saw her lean in and whisper something to Joanne, a nighttime regular.

"What'd she say?" he shouted. Joanne looked at him. Rhonda walked out from behind the bar to collect glasses.

"Fuck you," he shouted to Joanne. "It ain't none of your goddamn business."

Applesauce stopped playing pinball and walked over. What's-the-Point followed closely behind him.

Butterchurn said, "You should get on. Go to our house if you ain't going home. The RV ain't locked."

"I thought you was my friend? Now you kicking me out?" Milt looked at Applesauce who blocked Milt from the view of the other patrons. "And what the hell are you over here for, you damn mute?"

Applesauce looked at Butterchurn.

"Cut it out, Milt," Butterchurn said. "Let's just step outside for some air then."

"Fuck you. I wanna drink. And I'm gonna get one if I gotta jump across this goddamn bar and get it myself." He stood up. Butterchurn put his hand on his shoulder and pressed him back down. Everyone in the bar stopped what they were doing to watch.

"Get your goddamn hands off me."

Butterchurn did. Milt stood back up and Applesauce put his hand on his shoulder. Milt swung at him, but was too slow and Applesauce countered, knocking Milt to the ground.

"What'd you go and do that for?" Butterchurn asked him.

"Meant to knock him out," Applesauce said. He had a way of talking that if you weren't looking for it you'd think his lips never moved.

Milt looked up from the ground. "I always knew you were a piece of shit. You fucking mute. You fucking retard."

"Fuck him," Applesauce said to Butterchurn. "Let him go." He turned around and went back to his pinball machine.

Milt stood back up. "Walk away. You fucking faggot," he shouted.

"Let's go," Butterchurn said.

"I don't need you either," Milt said and left on his own accord. His left eye was reddening and beginning to swell shut.

"Did you get his keys?" Rhonda asked Butterchurn when he sat back at the bar, but it was too late.

Milt hit two cars and knocked over Butterchurn's bike on his way out the parking lot.

Milt pulled up to his trailer and slammed on the brakes just before running through it. Peggy opened the door to look out, and when she saw Milt charging toward her, she closed it and latched the door shut.

"Open the goddamn door, Peg." He pounded on the door. "I swear to God, if you don't open the fucking door, you're gonna be sorry. Open the fucking door." He kicked it. "Ain't you supposed to be at work, anyway? You got someone in there, don't you? Who are you fucking, Peg?"

He walked back to the truck. Peggy opened a window while he was next to the truck and threw out two duffle bags full of clothes. He rummaged through the toolbox in the bed of the truck until he found the hatchet and then walked back to the house.

"You're gonna get it now," he shouted.

"I'm calling the cops, Milt," she shouted through the door.

He smashed the hatchet through the door with one swing. Peggy shouted for help. He hit the door again, this time closer to the handle, where he meant to hit the first time, and the door flung open. Peggy yelled and huddled herself in the corner of the kitchen. She held a steak knife in her hand, but did not look prepared to use it. Milt stood over her with the hatchet raised. Peggy cried out and covered her face with her free hand. He kicked the knife out of her hand and spit on her. The hatchet rested on his right shoulder.

"I want you to see this. I want you to see how much I love you. And you never believed me. Look at me," he shouted. "Look at me."

She lowered her hand from her face, looking at him as if she accepted that this time he really meant to kill her. This time, he wasn't just threatening her. He swung the hatchet down. She didn't even scream and the hatchet stuck into the counter above her head.

"I told you I loved you." He began to laugh.

He opened the cabinet above the counter and grabbed a half bottle of whiskey. He unscrewed the cap and poured some in his mouth.

He stopped at the door before he left, still laughing. He turned to look at her one last time. "See how much I love you. I could've killed you, but didn't," he said and left.

He picked up the duffle bags and threw them in the bed of his truck and sped off. He drove down a dirt road, heavily wooded on either side and brought his truck to a stop when he felt he was far enough in that no one would bother him.

He turned the truck off, but kept the key turned, leaving the radio on. He turned up the volume and sang along to George Jones's "Tennessee Whiskey." When the song ended he stepped out of the truck to relive himself and tripped over the tracks. He forgot he parked on the railroad tracks, but quickly remembered why.

"I'll be damned," he said. "This is it."

He got the duffle bags out of the bed and went in front of the truck. If he continued down the road a bit farther, he would get to the little clearing that was a familiar spot with the high-school kids. He used to bring Peggy there when they first started dating. He brought his first wife here, too. Jenny, his high-school sweetheart. As a matter of fact, he thought, this was where Suzy was conceived. Suzy was his sixteen-year-old daughter that he had with Jenny, but hadn't seen either in nearly five years. Last he knew, Jenny went to jail for crystal meth possession and prostitution. And Suzy was living with Jenny's parents.

He threw the duffle bags to the ground, set the bottle by his feet, and pissed on the bags. Then got out a cigarette, lit it with a match, and threw the still flaming match on the bags. They didn't catch. He picked up the bottle, took a sip and poured a little on the soiled bags, threw his half-smoked cigarette on them and they caught. He watched as the flames rose. He took a pull, swished it around, and spit onto the burning bags watching the flames burn hotter. He took a longer pull, feeling his chest warm. He let out a howl and stomped his feet to the music that blared from his truck. He put his free hand to his mouth and hit his lips, making the Indian sounds he used to when he was a kid. He danced around the fire, pouring the whiskey down his throat, and spilling some down his shirt. He poured some over his face. He gargled with it. The whole time doing some odd, pagan dance.

The music stopped, so he stopped dancing and looked over at his truck, the headlights dimming.

"We gather here today," he said. "To celebrate the end of the saga of the great Milt Andrews." He thought back to when he was a child and he would go to church with his grandmother.

"The passing of a worthless father and a cocksucker of a husband. An asshole of a friend," he continued. I can't believe I took a swing at Applesauce, he thought. I was such a dick to Rhonda, too. And Butter. They were my only friends.

"Lord, may you save this damned soul from the raptures of hell," he said aloud. "May you lift his spirits to your paradise and forgive him all he has done on this hell we call Earth." My daughter barely knows her father. I hope she doesn't grow up to be as fucked up as I am because of it.

"God, we gather here today to ask you to rid this earth of one more evil. Let us make this place a safer one, a friendlier one, for those that come after us. Let them not know the horrors we know." I wonder if I could still make things right.

He lifted the bottle to his lips. Some liquid poured into his mouth, but he held it there without swallowing. It's not too late. I'm only forty-three. He spit it out. I could reform. I could make things better. He put his hands to his eyes, fell to his knees, and began to cry. Letting out every ounce of suffering that he experienced since childhood. His eighth birthday when he walked into the shed to find his father's brains splattered against the work bench. When his mother remarried only a year later to another abusive drunk. He cried all of it out.

He threw the bottle as far as he could. He lifted his hands and head to the sky, the tears shimmering on his face off the fire's glow as the headlights faded out.

"God, forgive me," he cried. "And God help me. I don't wanna die. I wanna make sure my daughter is taken care of. I wanna provide like a father's supposed to. I wanna break the cycle. I know I…"

A train whistle broke him from his prayer, the first prayer he said in thirty-five years.

He ran back to the truck. The battery, dead. The train light shone from around the bend and the whistle grew louder. He put the truck in neutral and tried to push it, but he didn't have the strength to get the back tires over the tracks.

He watched the impact from the safety of the woods and saw the train buckle after the collision, his truck no longer looking like a truck. He didn't think that the train would have jumped the track. The plan was for his own destruction. He wasn't supposed to kill anyone else. Why did God save him and not the three crew members who each had families? The prayer he thought was answered by salvation was only a confirmation to the black futility of the only life he ever knew.

Milt said one last prayer for forgiveness and wrapped the sheet tightly around his neck. The other end of the sheet was tight on the upper rung of the top bunk. He thought the other three cellmates were asleep. But the guy on the top bunk opposite him peered with one eye open as Milt dropped to a crouch as low as he could go and then leaned forward using his body weight to end his own life.

Southern Cross

Hank Ackerman stood outside the convenience store, having just spent his last three dollars on a tall boy and a scratch off. He was trying to hold off the realization that he was back on the verge of homelessness, something he hadn't experienced since he was growing up in Sullivan, Florida. Spring was a few weeks away. If he did have to sleep on the street, it wouldn't be too cold.

He set the beer on the window ledge and scratched the lottery ticket. Fifty dollars. The universe didn't completely hate him, he thought. He sat on the curb and bummed a cigarette and a light from a kid walking by with too many tattoos and too many piercings. He took a pull of the beer and a long slow drag of the cigarette. The night was damp and the moon shone through the misty haze. If he could find some work in the next couple of days, it was still possible to pull out of the tailspin. Two weeks without a paycheck was embarrassing, but there just wasn't much work around, not for someone with his record. Construction was slow and the bigger commercial companies could hire kids straight out of trade school for pennies. Hell, he'd work for pennies.

He looked at the ticket in his hand. Fifty dollars wasn't going to pay his rent next month. He took another drag of the cigarette and put it out to save the other half for later. He'd gotten really good at rationing. He cashed the ticket and was convinced things were turning around.

If he would've just rode his bike back to the house without thinking about his ex-wife telling him she was planning on moving seven states away with their three-year-old kid, he would've been good. He pedaled faster, trying to sweat out his anger, but as he passed by Sharky's Tavern, he stopped for a drink. Smokers huddled around the doorway with a yellow light beyond them and he imagined the hours of jovial, light-hearted banter that he could engage in with strangers, people who had no idea how fucked up his life had become in the last four years. The force that dragged him in there was irresistible. That's what he told himself anyway. But the truth was that he was afraid to go home and have that god-awful thought again. He used to think no matter how down on his luck he was, he would never do it. But lately, he started to think differently. He started thinking there was no other way.

He couldn't believe she was willing to take his boy away from him like that. He busted his ass for the first three years of his life to be the best father he could and was even willing to carry on with a woman that he slowly, but more recently, very rapidly, grew apart from to give his son a better life. He knew she was fucking around, but didn't think she would leave him, at least not for a twenty-four-year-old kid that worked as a goddamn secretary in the dental office. He could've handled it if she just had an affair with him. He'd thought of affairs many times. Probably would've had one if the situation ever arose. An affair was understandable. But he wanted to be there for his kid. He wanted him to have a father. And she knew that. She knew how important it was to him. He guessed she figured since the affair didn't piss him off, she had to do something more drastic.

He rode into the parking lot, feeling the eyes of the younger folks judging him for showing up on a bicycle. It was cool if they rode bicycles because they were being hip. But for him, a middle-aged dude showing up in a rusted-out Schwinn that he picked up at the flea market for twenty dollars showed them that he wasn't riding it to be cool or for any environmental reasons. It was his transportation. After locking up the bike he walked by and said hello as he entered the bar. Two girls looked away. One guy acknowledged him with a head nod.

There was a spot at the bar in the corner by one of those game machines that allowed you to circle what was wrong on the picture of naked chicks. Years ago, old folks hung out there and people would smoke inside and fill up the requests on the jukebox to listen to classic rock and dance until near closing time when they would switch it to the heartbreak country songs. Now, the college kids took over. They thought the Schlitz signs were neat and retro. You weren't even allowed to smoke inside anymore.

He thought if there were a jukebox he would've played "Up on Cripple Creek." He could always find someone to dance with when that song was played. That one or "Southern Cross." Rose would never dance with him, and she would get so pissed when he'd get up and dance with another woman. She got pissed about everything though: the type of beer he drank, the way he ate tacos, how he farted in his sleep. As if he could help such a thing. Sure, there were things he didn't care for that she did, but he was willing to deal with it. He was willing to deal with how she ordered medium-well steak and over-cooked burgers and how she bitched when there was too much salt around the rim of her Margarita or even how she would never have sex with him when they showered together because it wasted too much water. He was willing to sacrifice those things. Maybe tonight he would find a drunken broad who felt as low as he did and they could fuck their sorrows away for a few days. It had been so long he wasn't sure if his dick still worked.

On his third Pabst Blue Ribbon, he still hadn't found the woman he was looking for. He hadn't approached any either. He said hello to the young little thing that squeezed next to him and rubbed her tit on his shoulder as she ordered a purple shot of something, but she kind of scrunched up her eyebrows and said hello like she didn't know if he was really talking to her. After that, he just stared at the basketball game on the TV while imagining banging the sexy barmaid. Her breasts were trying to jump out of her V-neck and land right in his face. She caught him looking a time or two, and she gave a sideways glance. He smiled and lowered his head. Instead of talking to her, he would just ask for another beer.

"Put that on my tab," he heard a familiar voice behind him say. "I think I owe ol' Hank some money anyway."

It was Rodney Helms. Rodney Motherfucking Helms.

"Haven't seen you in a while," Rodney said. "How's life treating you?"

"Not sure you really want an honest answer."

Hank stood up and Rodney gave him a hug.

"How about Teddy? Talk to him any?"

Hank shook his head no.

"Hey buddy," Rodney said to the guy next to Hank, "Mind if I have this seat. I haven't seen my friend here in a long time."

"I'm sitting with my wife," the guy said. Rodney turned his back to the guy.

"Fucking assholes," Rodney said. "They're everywhere. Can I get a White Russian?" he said to the barmaid when she looked his way. The guy next to him looked as if he wanted to say something, but his wife shook her head. She looked a bit nervous.

The barmaid set Rodney's drink down, a little froth of half and half spilling over the side and Rodney said, "Let's grab that booth over there," and he pointed to the one in the back corner. "I got an idea you might like. It was fate that I happened onto you tonight."

"Fate, huh? Fuck fate."

"That bad, huh?"

They walked over. A young kid was setting up his things for an acoustic set at the front of the bar.

"So, you been down and out?" Rodney asked.

"Seems like you only come around when I fuck up."

"How are you, and what's your wife's name again?"

"Rose. She moved out about four months ago." Hank looked around the bar. He didn't want to talk to anyone about it. Especially not Rodney.

"Wait. Didn't you guys have a kid?"

Hank nodded. "Remember that day I came out on your boat and dove for the anchor?"

Rodney said he didn't. "Should I?"

"Probably not."

"You guys divorced?"

Hank shook his head. "I haven't signed the papers."

"Ha," Rodney nearly shouted. "So, how's the kid?"

"Great, I guess. I'm not allowed to see him." Hank took a long pull of his beer. A waitress walked by, and he waived her down. "Can I get a whiskey on the rocks?"

Rodney ordered another White Russian.

"On my tab. You switch to whiskey, ya?"

"Fucking right."

"You hadn't changed."

Hank smiled. "Not sure it was in my cards. Even if I tried," he said. "And shit, man, did I try. There was a time when I thought my life wouldn't have led me to where I am now. Thought I had what it took to get out, you know? Now, I'm not so sure I ever had a chance. Failing is so goddamn easy and always right around the corner. There was a time when I believed in a world that still had dreams in it, and people could accomplish those dreams. Now, not so much. I think everyone is living in denial. Believing the lies. Makes life bearable, you know? But I think we are doomed from the start."

"Speak for yourself. Life has been pretty kind to me. I was one of the lucky ones, I guess."

"I know you are, Rodney. You always were. But some of us just can't catch a fucking break."

"Why ain't you allowed to see your boy, Hank?"

"Long story."

"I heard about it. Is it true?"

"Whatja hear?"

"You tried to run someone over. Your wife's lover."

"That's bullshit."

"What's the story then?"

Hank shook his head. "DUI. Was never charged with the assault. But it's…it's fucked up is what it is."

"Jesus, man. You and Teddy were always some sorry motherfuckers, weren't you?"

Hank could only laugh. "I'm starting to think so."

Rodney laughed. "I'm just fucking with you."

"What's been up with you?" Hank said.

"Business as usual."

Hank thought back to when he first started working on boats with Rodney and how that was maybe the most enjoyable time of his life. He only quit working on boats when he fell in love, a word that obviously meant something different to his wife, he thought. After marriage, Hank went to school and became a teacher.

Rodney, on the other hand, after inheriting his grandmother's money and house, sold sunglasses on the island and eventually sold that business to his buddy Earl. He then sold the house, lived in a sailboat, and sat at the poker tables over at the dog track nearly every day.

"Shit's still going good for you, huh?" Hank asked.

"More money than I know what to do with. Shit, won eight hundred at the tables today, just fucking around."

"Sounds horrible."

"Can't lose if I try."

"I could show you how."

"Don't. I have no idea what you did in a past life, but I want no part of it."

"Hate to see what I come back as in the next."

Hank's whiskey showed up. His first whiskey since the incident. He swore it off, but he could feel the veins begin to pulse in his neck. Just thinking about his wife got his blood going.

"I gotta step out and get a smoke," Hank said.

"I'll come out with ya. I got a bit of herb if you want to smoke that?"

"I do."

They walked outside through the group of kids and toward the corner of the building away from everyone. Hank took his half of a cigarette out of his shirt pocket. Rodney looked at it and shook his head, then took out a joint from his cigarette pack.

"You got a light?" he asked.

Hank shook his head.

"Hey, one of you let me borrow a light," Rodney shouted as he started walking toward the group of kids. He lit the joint while standing between them. One of the kids asked if he could hit it since they let him borrow a light.

"Not now," Rodney said. He took a hit from it as he walked back over to Hank and handed it to Hank who took a deep hit, holding it in as long as he could, letting out a cough he hadn't felt in ages.

"How about this weather?" Rodney said.

"I don't mind it one bit." The fog was so thick the night sky looked orange from the moon trying to shine through.

All the cars were wet with the mist that swirled around.

They finished the joint and Hank lit his cigarette with the roach.

"I'll see ya in there when you're done," Rodney said.

Hank nodded.

Rodney walked back to the bar and before entering asked the kid if he wanted the roach. Rodney gave it to him and Hank sat smoking his cigarette watching them pass around the tiny roach, and then one kid burned his fingers on it and dropped it. The others gave him hell for it.

After his cigarette, Hank thought of leaving. Rodney's good fortune was starting to piss him off, but maybe if he hung out with him, some of it might rub off. Fuck it, he thought, maybe some of his bad luck would rub off on Rodney. Either way, couldn't hurt to hear him out. And free booze. He wasn't in a position to turn down free anything.

Back in the bar, Rodney had already ordered two more drinks.

"So, what's this idea you've got?" Hank asked, sitting down.

The kid with the guitar was playing and Rodney yelled up at him as he finished the song, "Play something we know."

"What would you like, sir?" the kid responded, obviously a bit perturbed to have an old man yell out at him.

"You know any Lovett?"

"You mean, like, Lyle Lovett?" the kid said into the microphone.

There was a chuckle throughout the bar.

"No. Not *like* Lyle Lovett. I actually want to hear you

play a Lyle Lovett song."

"All I know is 'If I had a Boat,'" the kid said.

"Perfect. Play that sumbitch."

Rodney took a drink of his White Russian and licked the milky liquid from his mustache and said, "I've been spending the last two weeks preparing to head out. I'm all set. I'll leave tomorrow, if you say let's go. I need someone to sail with me. And it's gotta be someone I can tolerate. I've grown to like you, Hank. You are an alright dude. And shit, you don't have anything going for you here."

"Where you going?" Hank asked.

"Spend some time down in Key West. Then Bahamas. Then wherever. I'm leaving for good."

"How long are you going?"

"What part of 'leaving for good' didn't you understand? I'm not coming back. I've got enough money to last two lifetimes."

"Must be nice."

"You are goddamn right it is. Anyone says money can't buy happiness, ain't ever had any money. We just gotta get you a passport."

"I have one. Went to Mexico two years ago. Thought a vacation would help us get close again."

"Did it?"

"Fuck no. We argued the entire time. It was the longest six nights of my life. Tell ya the truth, I think she fucked a bartender while we were there."

"Jesus, man."

"But I can't go. I gotta get a job. I'm gonna have to make

my way to fucking Missouri as soon I can. That's where she's moving to. As soon as this damn restraining order gets lifted and I can see my boy. I gotta get my shit together. I can't leave my boy for that long."

"Well, I'm going. I'm about to just go by myself, but I don't want to do that. I really need you."

"I can't."

"What do you have to lose? Come on. Key West, Cuba, Grand Caymans, Cancun, you name it. What do you say?"

It sure as hell sounded tempting. Hank ran his fingers through his hair and looked at the gray strands that came out and hung between his fingers.

"You don't have to pay for anything," Rodney said.

"Good. I don't have any money."

"I'll hire you out for room and board. I just don't want to sail down there alone. Hell, besides room and board, I'll give you two hundred a week spending money. You can fly home and see your boy when the order is up."

"How about I think about it and talk to you tomorrow?"

"I might be gone. I've got to get outta here. Glad I ran into you though. You good?"

Hank nodded.

"You aren't going, are you?" Rodney asked and finished his drink.

Hank smiled.

"If you change your mind, I've been keeping my boat parked down by the Bayfront Auditorium."

"I'll think about it."

Hank took a sip of the whiskey. He was getting pretty

drunk and thought about it. Stop at the different ports for a night and go into the bars on a tear. Hang out in Key West for a few days. Grab a fish sandwich at BO's Fish Wagon. Have a frozen piece of Key Lime Pie on a stick covered in chocolate. Shoot some pool at Capt. Tony's. Shake the old man's hand if he was still alive. Get a little snorkeling in. Maybe meet a couple of girls looking for an adventure down there. Boats work wonders with the ladies.

They'd catch their own lobster and spear fish for Grouper and Mahi-Mahi. After Key West, they'd slide on down into Cuba in the middle of the night and pay off the dock keepers to keep quiet. He'd heard the whores in Havana were the best. The girls they would bring from Key West would stay on the boat while he and Rodney went on a jaunt through town like Hemingway and whatever guest he had down at the Finca. Hank used to read the hell out of *Islands in the Stream* and *Old Man in the Sea* when he was young and on the water. They would probably get into a few fights while down there just for the hell of it. Just to prove they still had it in them. To prove they could still hold their own. Get a few boxes of cigars and some Havana Club rum for the sail into the Green Flash.

After they were out of sight of Cuba they would hear a cat meow. The girls would've smuggled one on for a pet. They would name it Flotsam or Jetsam in honor of John Caldwell and his *Desperate Voyage*. That was another book he used to go through on those long three or four day trips on the water. And then on into the Caymans. Maybe find some work down there. Take tourists out on sunset sails. Serve them wine and cheese. Tell them stories of his adventures. When they had enough of that town, six maybe nine months later, they could decide to go home or keep the dream going. Who were they kidding? They wouldn't go home. They would never go back home.

By that time they would have become accustomed to being pirates. It was their calling. The girls by then would have either gotten tired of their drunk, old asses or they would have gotten tired of the girls bitching about them being old and drunk and having limp dicks. If the girls didn't leave first, Hank and Rodney would sail away one night while the girls were out with the local studs. They'd keep the cat of course. Maybe they would have even gotten another by then.

Then they'd either sail across the Gulf to Mexico and down the coast of Central America or stay within the Caribbean. The beauty of it would be that it didn't matter. Nothing would matter anymore. Hank would have a beard down to his bronzed chest and it'd be his shift for sailing and Rodney would be down in the cabin sleeping with the cats curled around his feet. Hank would be out under the stars sipping on a Rum Runner and missing his boy. Hopefully by then the idea of not being able to watch him grow up would have either become bearable or his heart would have become calloused. He'd write him a few letters and send him postcards from the different ports-of-call. His boy could collect stamps from all the different countries and would think his old man was an adventurer. Hank would still be Hank, but in his boy's mind Hank would be something much cooler. A lot cooler than that goofy wannabe dentist clown his boy probably already called daddy. The jackass who drove around in a BMW paid for by Hank's wife.

And I'm the bad guy, Hank thought, for sitting in my pickup truck drinking whiskey when I was supposed to be at work. And I'm the bad guy when this piece of shit son-of-a-bitch is inside my house fucking my wife. I'm the bad guy for pretending to run him over. It would've been funny as hell if my neighbor's Toyota wouldn't have been in my way. Jesus-Fucking-Christ. That would've been funny. But as it turned it out, it was not funny. Fucking bullshit is what it was.

Hank downed his drink and stumbled out of the bar to the sound of the kids out front laugh as he struggled to unlock the bike. He never pedaled so hard in his life and he threw up twice on the way to his trailer. Only thing he grabbed was his passport. He was back on the bicycle and pedaled hard for another twenty minutes until he pulled up into the old neighborhood.

He rode slowly as he approached his old house, trying not to make a sound.

The lights were off in Braden's room. Hell, he had no idea what time it was. There was that BMW attached to the moving truck. The lights were on in the living room. He ditched the bike across the street, snuck through the neighbor's yard, hopped the fence in the front yard of his old house, and crawled through the bushes to sit underneath Braden's window. He was still out of breath and sweating. He could hear his own breathing, and it donned on him how loud he was being. He calmed his breathing and crouched up on his haunches to peer through the window.

The blinds made a slight slit through which to observe the interior of the room. A nightlight shone. Braden always slept with the lights on. There was nothing in his room except his bed. Everything else was packed. And Hank could almost make out Braden's beautiful person lying in the bed. All Hank wanted was to tell him bye, give him a hug. Tell him he'd see him soon. Tears blurred his vision. He knew there was no way in hell, even if he asked nicely, that she would allow him to say goodbye to Braden. Hank tried lifting the window and wondered if they fixed that window in the spare bedroom. He used to be able to wiggle that thing open. He went around to the back yard, jumped the fence, and scooted close to the house until he was underneath the spare bedroom window. It lifted without much effort. He lifted it just half way and stuck his head inside. The room was empty. He listened and could hear the TV on in the living room. He took off his shoes, so as not to track mud through the house, and climbed through the window, tiptoeing quietly to the door to peer out into the hallway. He could see his wife and that kid lying on the floor under a blanket watching TV. For a moment, Hank thought of sneaking up on them and doing a Hulk Hogan leg drop across them both. Instead, he walked down the hallway. Braden's door was shut. "When did he start sleeping with the door shut?" Hank thought and turned the door handle slowly.

"Did you hear that?" Rose said.

Hank stopped and held his breath.

"Braden? Is that you? Go back to bed, little man."

Who the fuck is he calling his little man? Hank thought before turning the knob again even slower than the previous time, and as the door opened it made a loud screech.

"Braden, what is it?" Rose said and stood up.

Hank thought of hiding in the closet or the bathroom or somewhere. But if they found him, he wouldn't be able to say bye. In his drunken, desperate mind it was better to give him a hug and say bye now and just get caught. He rushed in, lifted him up and hugged him harder than he ever hugged anyone before.

"Daddy?" Braden said.

Hank started crying and managed to say, "I love you, little dude. Don't ever forget that."

"What the fuck?" Rose said as she saw Hank kneeling by the bed with Braden in his arms.

Hank let go of Braden, slowly turned to her and said, "Rose just let me explain."

She turned on the light. Hank looked back at Braden. His blond hair had gotten long. He looked so beautiful. "Just wait a minute, please," Hank said again. He wiped the tears away with the back of his hand.

"Jarrod, call the cops," Rose said. "You're fucking drunk," she said to Hank. "Where the fuck are your shoes?"

"What is it, babe?" the voice from the living room said as Jarrod ran down the hallway and when he came to the room and saw Hank, he said, "You motherfucker" and stood at the door in shock.

Hank looked over at Braden who was rubbing his eyes trying to make sense of the senseless.

"I fucked up bad," Hank said, whether to Braden or Rose or himself was unclear. "Not just tonight, but this poor kid's whole life. I wasn't the father I thought I would be. Maybe my dad knew that as well. No matter how bad you want it, some people are just toxic. I didn't want to be the toxin that ruined this beautiful boy, yet here I am. I'm sorry."

Hank stood up and put his hands up. "I'm sorry. I just wanted to say bye one last time."

"Jarrod," Rose said, "Don't just stand there. Call the goddamn cops."

Jarrod didn't call the cops. Instead, he charged at Hank and Hank punched him in the throat and dropped him to the ground. He had never done that to anyone before, but always thought if he had to that was where he was going to aim.

"I'm sorry, buddy," Hank said again, this time directly to Braden.

Rose screamed and came at him. Braden cried out "Daddy." Hank froze for a moment. He didn't know if Braden was calling for him or Jarrod.

Hank didn't even realize he'd pushed Rose down until he was past her and out the front door. He ran across the street to the bike and pedaled as hard as he could. He couldn't go home. He couldn't ever go home and he damn sure wasn't going to jail. Not for wanting to say bye to his boy.

It took him about fifteen minutes of pedaling to get to the docks and Rodney was already asleep, but Hank brought his bike on board and woke him up.

"Let's go," Hank said.

"What? What are you talking about?"

"You want to go sailing. Let's go. Right now."

"You're drunk."

"A little. Get up and let's go. Right fucking now."

Rodney shot straight up out of his bed. "What did you do?"

"I fucked up. Bad. You gotta help me."

"What did you do?"

Hank told him.

"Holy shit. You fucked up."

Hank never looked at somebody with such desperation before.

"I can't just up and leave," Rodney said.

"You said you were all ready."

"I am. But…"

"But what? What are you waiting on? Have you ever even been out of the Intercoastal before on this thing?"

Rodney shook his head.

"I'm begging you. Let's do this. If not, I'm going to jail. I don't want to go to jail. I won't go to jail."

Rodney looked at Hank and knew Hank was in a bad way. Rodney knew what Hank thought was his only other option.

"Hand me those jeans."

Hank picked up the jeans from off the couch across from where Rodney lay and handed them to him.

"Fuck, man. I guess we are going to do it, huh?" Rodney said and pulled on his jeans.

"Yes. Yes, we are," Hank said.

"Let's untie and get moving."

Hank hurried to the deck and took off the sail covers, Rodney untied from the cleats, and they pushed off in the thickest fog Hank ever saw. Visibility was nearly zero, and it didn't take long for the docks to fade from sight. Hank went below deck and Rodney set the course.

When Hank woke, they were anchored outside of Panama City Beach. Rodney was drinking a cup of coffee.

"Hell of a night, huh?"

Hank hung his head. "Sorry, man."

"Sorry nothing. You got me moving."

Rodney poured Hank a coffee.

"I'm going to take the dinghy into shore and get a few supplies. We are sailing open water from here to Tampa. Stay a day, maybe two in Tampa, and then open water from Tampa to Key West. How long before you think it'll blow over and you can go back?"

Hank pulled his passport from his jacket pocket.

"You planned this?"

"Not the getting caught part."

Rodney finished his coffee and set off for the supply run. Hank sat out on the deck, and the only thing that he could think was that he didn't have the address in Missouri to send postcards to his boy and that was a good thing. It was best if Braden never heard from Hank again. As much as Hank loved him, the best thing he thought he could do was not be in his life. He seemed to always find a way to fall backward, and he didn't want to pass that on any further. He wanted to break the curse. He would pretend the water cleansed him. He would invent a game that only he played to help him forget about his past, a game in which he was the hero. He would join the other expatriates, and they could tell lies to one another.

Merle

"Can't believe they hadn't found ol' Cotton's boy yet," Merle said. He took off his ragged captain's hat and scratched the crusty scabs on his balding head.

"Yeah, it doesn't look good," said George.

"Wonder how Cotton's handling it," Merle said and then slid his queen across the board. "Check mate."

"Aw. You sumbitch. Got me again, didja?" George slowly rose from his wicker chair. His shirt clung to his back from the sweat, and he adjusted it before grabbing his cane, which was hung on the wall next to where they sat on the porch nearly every day and limped off inside Lenny Jr.'s convenience store.

Lenny Jr.'s store was once a pharmacy and soda fountain that his late daddy, Lenny Sr., owned. Lenny Sr. was good friends with Merle, George, and Cotton and was the pharmacist of Sullivan, Florida. Merle and George were both veterans of the Korean War and worked together down in Gulf Shores. Cotton wasn't a fisherman. His grandfather owned about two-hundred acres of pine fields and then after clearing the land of lumber turned that land into cotton fields. When Cotton inherited it, his old man already sold off most of it. Cotton did the same and was now down to about 15 acres. When Lenny's was still a pharmacy, the three old men would stop by and Lenny Sr. would give them a taste of that special medicine he always kept around. Some of the town folk called it whiskey, others called it moonshine, but Lenny Sr., Merle, George, and Cotton called it medicine.

After pharmacies and soda fountains became outdated, Lenny Sr. decided to cash in on the oil companies and converted his store into a gas station. He sold some necessities like eggs, milk, and beer. But he always supplied his buddies with his own homemade medicine. He had one gas pump out front that hardly got used. Even in a town of fifteen hundred people, it seemed as if Lenny's was left behind. The town peaked at thirty-two hundred citizens in the 1930s, but when lumber left, so did the people. Without people, the stores boarded up their windows.

After Lenny Sr. passed away from a brain aneurism, Lenny Jr., who served in the Army and fought in Vietnam, came back to run the family business. It rarely saw a customer except old Merle and George. They seemed to be the only reason the place stayed open. But Lenny Jr. built a little place out back to live in and decided that he was going to run Lenny's until he died. Since he didn't have any kids himself, he didn't care what happened to it once he was gone. He felt it had a good run and was now ready to fade away and become another abandoned lot. He built a barn a little further back, and he was known to host cockfights, dogfights, and even some boxing matches.

"Any new word yet on Cotton's boy?" George asked Lenny Jr. who sat behind the counter in a rusted lawn chair with a cigarette butt about to the filter in one hand and a can of beer in the other. He watched the car races on a thirteen-inch black and white television that showed a snowy picture more often than a clear picture.

"Naw. They still looking. But I heard there was some

blood spots on the carpet next to a dental plate. Says it was Hippie's, his girlfriend. They saying foul play could be involved. I think they just making stuff up, though. Who knows? They were messed up folk anyways."

"How you gonna say that? Wasn't Cowboy a friend of yours?"

"More like acquaintances. Not much in common. He dodged, I served. And didn't even have the decency to help out his old man with the fields. Look at Cotton now, ain't got a damn thing to show for that long life he lived."

"Who's winning?" George said trying to watch a bit of the race.

"Looks like Earnhardt."

"Knew he would. Told Merle that before the race started."

George limped away to the restroom. Lenny Jr. downed the rest of his beer, threw the can at the garbage pail but missed, then put his cigarette out in the ash tray – which had about thirty butts in it – and got out another one. Once it was lit, he sat back and grabbed another beer from the Styrofoam cooler sitting by his feet.

Although Lenny Jr. looked like a cowboy, his nickname wasn't Cowboy. That's what everyone called Cotton's boy.

"Get us some more medicine, wouldja?" George said as he came from the bathroom.

"Why the hell you still calling it medicine? Everyone knows what it is you two drink out there. They always knew."

"We call it medicine cause that's what it is. You ever hear me cough?"

"Where's your jars?"

"Outside."

"You want clean ones, I suppose?"

"We really gotta do this every day? Your daddy always gave us clean jars."

"Let Daddy get you clean ones then."

George shook his head and limped off to get the mason jars, mumbling under his breath. Before he got out of the door he started having a coughing fit. These fits usually lasted a couple of minutes, ending with him spitting out a wad of phlegm and drool dribbling down his chin. But he was tough and would overcome these fits and keep on his way like nothing happened.

Merle already had the chessboard set up again and a fresh cigar lit. He handed an unlit one to George who put it in his shirt pocket. He then grabbed a mason jar off the picnic table. He could only carry one because he couldn't walk a few steps without his cane.

He came back out with his mason jar filled to the rim and sloshing over the side with every step. Before he sat down, he poured half of the clear liquid into Merle's jar.

They each took a sip. Merle didn't make a face or shiver like George did. George bit off the end of his cigar, and then, as if it was a ritual, they dipped the ends of their cigars in the homemade whiskey, and while Merle made the same opening move as the last game, George lit his cigar. Both old men sat and played the game in silence puffing and sipping while the other contemplated the next move. The conversation wouldn't start back up until the last few moves of the game, which Merle usually won. George never gave up hope, though, because every once in a great while, he'd win. Merle would say he let him just to keep things interesting, but George would hoot and holler anyway. He'd tell Merle what a lousy player he was and ask him if he was stupid or something. Merle would just say something like, "Sit your old wrinkled ass down before I make you. And stop all that fussing." Lenny Jr. would usually come out just to make sure it didn't go any further because back in the day after a few swigs of medicine they were known to throw a few punches at each other. But it didn't happen so much anymore. Not since that time when George finally finished whittling that cane of his and smacked Merle in the shin with it, and Merle pulled a hunting knife that he kept on his hip and said if George were to ever do something stupid like that again, he wouldn't think twice to skin him like a doe. People didn't question Merle about things like that.

* * * *

Everyone knew or thought they knew about Merle's past. But no one was ever sure. Maybe George, Cotton, and Lenny Sr., but they wouldn't talk. When Merle was just a kid, eight or nine, his dad was killed. The law said his mom killed him in self-defense because his dad was always beating on her. She had bruise marks around her arms and all, but the story around town was different. The story was that Merle's dad was strangling his mom and about to kill her, so Merle grabbed the hunting knife that was on the table and stabbed his own dad in the back of the neck five or six times. They say when the cops showed up Merle and his momma were sitting on the couch, and Merle was still covered with his father's blood.

But there was also that story about his first wife and her lover. Merle married his high school sweetheart, Anita Whitmire, just before heading off to Korea, and when he came back four years later, she was running around with another boy. Well, they disappeared and Merle moved down to Gulf Shores to fish. The stories were that Merle killed them both and fed their bodies to the wild hogs out at the hunting grounds, but no bones were ever found. As a kid, Lenny Jr. would hear these stories and ask his pa if they were true, and Lenny Sr. would say that Merle was a good, God-fearing Christian and Christians didn't do things like that.

* * * *

George told Merle what Lenny Jr. said about Cotton's missing boy and how they weren't really friends. While he was talking he moved his rook and took Merle's last knight. Merle quickly swung his queen clear across the board, using the same exact move as the last game, and took the rook.

"Checkmate."

"You son-of-a-bitch. I'll be damned."

"No suspects yet, huh? What the hell they waitin on? Not that many people knew him. In the three days he been gone, they could've questioned everyone in the damn town."

At that time Sheriff Deputy Booker Latimer pulled up with Cotton sitting in the front seat. They put the mason jars under the tables.

"Gentlemen," Deputy Latimer said.

"Deputy," Merle said. George just nodded and looked

away. He wasn't too fond of Deputy Latimer because of all the times he was arrested for fighting and one time for an unspeakable act that no one ever could get Latimer to retell. George said he was blind drunk and couldn't remember.

"That piece-a-shit around?" Cotton said, walking up next to Latimer.

Lenny Jr. came out to the front. "I'm here, Cotton." His tone changed when he saw Latimer, "Deputy what brings you around?"

"Need to ask you some questions about Rex and June." June was the real name of Rex's girlfriend, the one everyone called Hippie.

"Didn't we talk about it yesterday?" Lenny Jr. said.

"We did, but Cotton has remembered something. He says you were the last to see them."

"What the hell does ol' Cotton know? His brain is just as wet as these two."

"Can we talk inside?" Deputy Latimer asked.

Lenny Jr. nodded. Although Lenny Jr. stood about six foot three, next to Latimer, he didn't look so tough. Cotton tried to follow them in, but Latimer told him it was best to wait outside.

Cotton sat down next to George on the bench.

"Give me a taste of that," he said. George looked around and handed him the jar. Cotton took a swallow. He didn't screw up his face, but he still shivered. Merle set the pieces back in place.

"I can get the next game?" Cotton asked.

"As soon as I whoop his ass," George said. Merle smiled

and Cotton laughed.

"I wanted to play today," Cotton said. George looked sideways at Cotton. Cotton took another swig.

"I got a bad feeling about Lenny Jr. Like he might know something," Cotton said.

"Why you say that?" Merle asked.

"Cause him and Rex weren't getting along too good as of late. Lenny Jr. had started coming in and telling Rex he owed him some money or something. You know they were mixed up with them drugs. Crank, I think I heard them call it, or something like that. I told Latimer that, too."

Merle smirked because he already saw the pattern and how he was going to checkmate George.

"You know, when I talk to Lenny Jr., he don't seem too upset that someone he knew for what, nearly forty years, turned up missing. Maybe it was the war made him like that though," George said.

"Why don't you check out his truck when me and Latimer leave? See if you notice anything unusual," Cotton said.

Merle nodded.

"I know he did something. Or he knows who did. And if I find out, I swear to God I'll kill that sumbitch."

"You don't know what you're talking about," Merle said.

"Bullshit, he done something to my boy. I'll kill that pigfucker. And I don't care who knows, neither."

"It takes a long time to get yourself straight after something like that, Cotton. And I don't know if you got enough time to live to work that out with who you gotta work it out with. Killing a man is hard to do. Don't want to die with that on your soul."

Latimer and Lenny Jr. walked out. Latimer saw the mason jars on the table and George tried to hide it, but the deputy said, "I got bigger things to worry about, George. You staying here, Cotton?"

"No." He looked at Lenny Jr. "Don't ever wanna see this boy's face again."

"Cowboy had a lot of enemies, Cotton. I ain't the only one wanted him dead." Latimer was already on his way to the car and didn't hear that last part.

"Your time's a coming," Cotton said and then left with Latimer.

Lenny Jr. sat down with the two old men. He took a sip out of George's jar.

"Cotton's done drank himself stupid thinking I'm involved with that shit." Lenny Jr. took another sip and took a deep breath, exhaling slowly. Merle watched him, studied him.

"George," Merle said, "why don't you leave us two alone for a minute?"

Lenny Jr. looked up at him.

"Can't we just finish this game?"

"Later George. I got something I need to talk to Junior about."

"What the hell could be more important...Oh yeah. You go on and talk, I'll be inside watching the race."

Lenny Jr. waited for George to be inside. "I don't know

what Cotton told you, Merle, but I didn't have nothing to do with it."

"It ain't me you gotta convince."

"I ain't gotta convince no one."

"Look, you think I hadn't been in your shoes before. Everyone in this town thinks they know what happened with my wife and that other guy."

"Dave?"

"Whatever his name was. What I mean is, you were just a kid then, but I'm sure you heard stories and came up with an opinion yourself."

Lenny Jr. nodded. "Pa always said don't worry about what other folks say. You a good man and that's all that matters."

"The point is that I had Latimer coming around every day harassing me. Now you gonna let Latimer's boy do the same to you?"

"I didn't do nothing."

Merle waited until the right words came to him. "I know. I didn't either."

"So, what do I do?" Lenny Jr. said. He pulled out of his pocket a little glass bullet that held the methamphetamine that Cotton talked about.

"You don't mind, do ya?" Lenny Jr. said.

Merle shook his head no. Lenny Jr. took a snort.

"Whatja do with the bodies?"

Lenny Jr. hesitated. "I uh… You ain't fooling me, old man."

"Don't be an idiot. You want help getting Latimer off

your back?"

Merle stared at Lenny Jr. until he understood.

Lenny Jr. then looked around nervously. "I took them out to the hunting club. By where Pa used to go. Near that pond. Where people say you…"

"It's a good spot. You bury them or threw them in the pond?"

"I uh…well see, I…I'd rather not say."

"Whatja do?"

"Well…I probably oughta show you."

* * * *

This was the third day in a row that Lenny Jr. came around looking for Cowboy, and every time he did so, Hippie would say he wasn't there. Always a different excuse. This time she said he was with Cotton. Lenny Jr. knew she was lying because he saw Cotton a few minutes ago sitting by himself in the cemetery where his wife was buried. This day, Lenny Jr. was going to get his money somehow or another. He wasn't thinking clearly either because he was on a three-day diet of crystal meth and whiskey. He needed the money even worse now.

When he came through the door, he pushed Hippie down. His eyes were bulging and couldn't focus on one spot for more than a quick second. The baseball bat in his hand told Hippie she was in trouble. Her mistake was getting up. She should have just stayed on the ground, but she tried to get rid of him. When she got close, Lenny Jr. swung. Her dental plate flew out and hit the wall on the other side of the trailer. The bat against the side of her head made such a hollow thud that Cowboy came out from hiding. He stood there with his cowboy hat on and boxer shorts and nothing else. Lenny Jr. didn't wait for Cowboy to react. He charged at him with such speed Cowboy didn't move until the bat crashed into his ribs and folded him in two. Lenny Jr. took the zip ties he brought along and fastened Cowboy's hands behind his back and his feet together. Then got a piece of duct tape and put over his mouth. Hippie was easy to carry, but Cowboy took some work. He took them back to his house in the bed of the truck. Cowboy was hurt badly and being ziptied, he posed no threat. He looked at Hippie and she was clearly dead. That was not part of the plan. He ran inside and grabbed a box of dynamite that was left over from his grandfather's days as a stump blaster and drove the thirty minutes to the three-hundred-acre hunting camp.

Not many people had a key to that land. In fact, out of all the old-timers, Lenny Sr. was the only one and he passed it down to Lenny Jr. The pond in the hunting grounds was a good hundred-acre drive through ruts and backwoods, and most people who hunted there never made it that far back. It was like Lenny Sr.'s own private paradise. Lenny Jr. didn't use it much since his old man had passed on.

At the pond, he dragged the bodies out onto the ground. He pulled the flask from his inside vest pocket and took a few swigs.

"I didn't mean to hit her so hard," he said to Cowboy. Cowboy squirmed a bit on the ground. "But she came at me, and it was the first thing I thought of. You know how that shit works your mind."

Lenny Jr. bent down and felt for a pulse. "She's dead." Cowboy squirmed more and let out an awful sound, worse than a piglet getting sliced open alive. "Shut up," Lenny Jr. said. "Shut up and let me think." He paced around a little. "I gotta kill you, now," he said to himself before turning to Cowboy, "She's dead. And I know you, Cowboy. You won't let this slide. We ain't that good of friends. Hell, you wouldn't even let me fuck her as a payback. If you would've just let me fuck her, none of this would've happened. I would've forgiven the debt."

He paced around some more. "Ain't nothing stoppin me from fucking her now though, is there?" At this, Cowboy grunted louder, and he continued squirming trying to break free of the zip ties.

Lenny Jr. walked over to Hippie. His eyes never left Cowboy's. He undid his pants and climbed on top of her, lifted her skirt, and ripped her underpants with a quick pull.

When he was done, he walked back to the truck, grabbed two sticks of dynamite, and placed one in Hippie's mouth.

He then ripped the duct tape off Cowboy's mouth and tried to shove one in there but Cowboy shouted so much and shook his head back and forth that Lenny Jr. couldn't get it in. He kicked him in the face to slow him down and then placed the tape back over his mouth.

"Well, since I can't get it in your mouth, there's only one other place." He yanked on Cowboy's boxer shorts until they ripped clean off. Cowboy squirmed trying to prevent the inevitable. Lenny Jr. managed to roll Cowboy over and shove it in deep enough so that he couldn't squeeze it back out. That didn't keep him from trying, though.

Then, with the extra fuse, he spliced together the dynamites so that he could get far enough away so as not to see the grand finale.

* * * *

"I heard the explosion as I was locking the gate back up," Lenny Jr. told Merle.

"What the hell's wrong with you, boy? Dynamite? My God." Merle took a hard pull of his drink. "As if killing them wasn't bad enough," he said.

"I just thought. You know, there wouldn't be anything left if I used dynamite. I wasn't thinking straight. Trust me, man. I hadn't been able to sleep since that shit."

"What about the bodies?"

"I don't know. I didn't wait to see."

"We gotta go out there."

"I can't go back."

"Gotta clean up that mess."

"When?"

"Tonight. Let it get dark a while. Maybe ten-thirty or eleven. I'll come back by."

Merle and George left Lenny Jr.'s. George tried to get Merle to tell him if he learned anything, but Merle told him all he needed to know.

At about eleven o'clock when most of the town was asleep and stars were shining bright in the darkness of a new moon, Merle went back to Lenny Jr.'s. Lenny Jr. sat in front of the television same as before, just a different cigarette and a different beer.

"Bout time you showed up, old man. I was getting to think you turned me in or something."

"You know I don't have no business with the law," Merle said. "The things we do in this life are between us and God. If we do wrong, all we can do is repent and let the Lord sort us out."

"Well, after I told you everything, I felt better about it. Thank you. I had to tell somebody. And I'm done with that shit, too. I flushed it all down the toilet as soon as you left."

"I don't have the power to absolve you, my boy."

"You're all I got though."

"I ain't nobody. I'd tell ya to get to church, but they ain't nobody either."

They got into Lenny Jr.'s rusted red pick-up truck that sat out back. When he came to a stop before pulling out of the parking lot, a wooden Louisville Slugger rolled forward. Merle glanced down and noticed the blood stains on it. He looked at Lenny Jr.

"I was wondering where that thing was."

Merle shook his head and looked out the window, pushing the bat back underneath the seat with his feet.

Merle didn't say a word on the drive to the hunting club. He dozed off a couple of times and woke up when he felt the truck stop. Lenny Jr. stepped out to unlock the fence.

They drove into the dark woods with only the fog lights running. When they got to the lake's edge, Lenny Jr. hit the bright lights so they could scan the entire landscape. Merle shook his head. Lenny Jr. got out of the truck, braced himself against the hood and heaved. He was not prepared for the smell. Merle got out of the truck holding the Louisville Slugger in his right hand. The sounds of the forest were overwhelmingly loud. Lenny Jr. came back to his senses when he heard a crackling in the darkness.

"You heard that?" he said looking up. "Why you got that bat, Merle?"

"You gotta get rid of it, too," Merle said. He walked around the front of the truck stepping over what looked like the remains of a torso. He couldn't really tell what any of it was. It looked like whatever was left after the explosion had been chewed on by wild beasts.

Lenny Jr. grabbed the shovel out of the bed of the truck. He started with the biggest piece first. He scooped up what he thought was the torso and carried it into the lake. After the plop, the crickets grew louder and an owl hooted. When he turned around, he saw George and Cotton standing beside Merle. George was holding a shotgun. Lenny Jr. wept.

"Stop crying, wouldja?" Merle said.

"Please, it was an accident," Lenny Jr. said. He threw down the shovel and dropped to his knees as the three old men approached him.

"You are one sick piece-a-shit," Cotton said.

Lenny Jr. tried to stop crying and stood up. "It was coming to him either way, Cotton." Merle sat him back down again with one quick, crushing swing to the knee. Lenny Jr. cried now for different reasons.

"Merle, you can't do this," he said through the tears.

"I'm not gonna," he said. George and Cotton looked at Merle. "I got nothing to do with this. But I do believe it's the right thing to do." He took his hunting knife from his hip holster and handed it to Cotton. "It was your boy. So, this is between you, Lenny Junior and God," Merle said to him.

"I told ya your time was a coming," Cotton said. He got down close and spat in Lenny Jr.'s face.

Cotton put the knife to Lenny Jr.'s throat. He hesitated. A trickle of blood came from where the knife was pressing into the skin. Cotton began in a barely audible tone reciting some kind of prayer. Lenny Jr. looked as if he accepted his sentence.

"Whatcha waiting on?" Merle said. "You wanna let the law sort it out?"

A couple more drawn out seconds passed.

"I can't do it," Cotton said. He brought the knife down. The tight grip he had on it turned his knuckles a yellow-white. He looked at George. George shook his head no.

"I didn't even really wanna come out here," George said.

"Let me go then. Living'll be suffering enough," Lenny Jr. said. "I really am sorry. It was that shit we were on. That's what it was. That shit's the devil. I was possessed and so was your boy." Merle lifted the bat to Lenny Jr.'s face sending him on his back. Lenny Jr. lifted his head displaying a bloody mouth and nose.

"Don't mention Cowboy at a time like this," Merle said. Turning to Cotton, "You gonna let him go then?"

"Nobody's gotta do anything," Lenny Jr. said. He sat up on his left elbow, his right hand cupping where he was hit, blood running between his fingers. "I'll turn myself in first thing in the morning."

"Won't do any good," Merle said. "God done saw it all."

"Oh no, Merle. Don't say that," Lenny Jr. said. Those were the dreaded final words all the kids ended their stories with when retelling the legend of Merle Bodine.

"What do you wanna do?" Merle said.

"I can't," Cotton said. He was weeping now. "I ain't got enough time left for the penance, like you said. But he shouldn't be allowed to walk around and pollute God's Earth."

Cotton squeezed the knife harder and took a deep breath, trying to muster up the courage.

"I'm sorry, Merle, but I can't," Cotton said again through the tears. Merle looked at George. George shook his head and walked to the truck. Cotton let the knife fall to the ground.

"Goddamn it," Merle said. "Why let the law get involved? We know he done wrong. He ain't leaving here alive. We have enough defective units in this world."

Lenny Jr. sat up and dropped his hand from his nose to push off the ground, but he never made it. In the moonless night, with only the woodlands and a few owls as honest witnesses, Merle picked up the knife, and as if bound by duty, killed a man.

The End

Acknowledgments

Thanks to my mom, Stella, and my beautiful daughter Zoë. You two keep my world normal. Thanks to Rick Canute and Izo Besares who read these stories in their very early drafts before I knew they would all work together as a novel and for encouraging me to keep making up stories. Thanks to Tony Eberhardt for helping edit all these stories before I sent it off to the Waldorf team.

Thanks to Dr. Josephs for pushing me to write more with less words. Thanks to Barbara Terry and the entire staff at Waldorf Publishing. Without them this book would still be hiding in my computer. Thanks to Julia Bonnabel Lippencott for being there when I needed someone to laugh with about how stupid the world is and for being an all-around great person. And a special thanks to all the strange people of the Florida Panhandle. We might live in paradise, but goddamn it if we don't always act like it.

Oh, and Tony Zupinski, how's that hand?

Author Bio

Nic Schuck was born in Pensacola, Florida. He graduated with a MA in English from the University of West Florida. Prior to earning his MA, Nic spent ten years as a public-school teacher. In 2012, he started his own business, Emerald Coast Tours, a historical tour company in Pensacola, Florida where he lives with his daughter and continues to lead tours. His debut novel, *Native Moments*, was published in 2016.

Also by
Nic Schuck

Native Moments, a novel

After the death of his brother, Sanch Murray leaves for a surf trip to Costa Rica as a way to cope, but also as a way to prolong making decisions about his adult life and sets out on a quixotic search for an alternative to the American Dream.

"Like the Walt Whitman lines from which Nic Schuck takes the title for his debut novel, *Native Moments* explores 'life coarse and rank' with its 'libidinous joys' and passions. With a keen ear for dialogue and a poet's eye for the resonate detail, Nic Schuck creates a world his readers will be eager to enter and reluctant to leave." **- Jonathan Fink, author of *The Crossing***

"Schuck does a good job of showing the multilayered cake that is Costa Rica, complete with surfing paradise, dangerous fauna, unlimited vice, all of which is coated in a sweet, ironic icing of Pura Vida. This is a great book to toss in your board bag on your next surf trip." **- Drew Sievers, TheWatermansLibrary.com**

Purchase on Amazon or anywhere books are sold.
Follow Nic Schuck on Facebook, Twitter or Instagram.